If he'd been her

been okay.

He would have...what? Dez wasn't a doctor. He was just a man who cared for her. Who would do anything to save her. But what could he do in this case? He took a seat in the chair beside Sherri's hospital bed and leaned his elbows on his knees. His head in his hands, he closed his eyes and took a shuddering breath.

He stood and pressed his lips against her forehead. "You have to fight this, my fierce warrior. Fight this and come back to me healthy and well." He kissed her again and listened to her soft breathing.

Sherri's mom whispered, "You love her." She said it as a statement, not a question.

Dez nodded and took Sherri's hand in his. Pressed his lips to it and watched her sleep. "Always."

Dear Reader,

As a breast cancer survivor, I am so excited to bring you the Hope Center Stories about three women who are on their own journeys with cancer. They will face their fears and celebrate their victories together because that's how we defeat this horrible disease: with the love and support of family, friends and medical staff. As long as we can hold on to each other, cancer cannot destroy us. It may damage and scar our bodies, but our faith and will to live will help carry us through.

Sherrita Lopez is about to start her own fight with breast cancer. For someone who prides herself so much on her independence, she is about to learn that the journey requires family and friends to support and love her through the difficult times. She also discovers that the friend who has always been by her side is the man she can't live without.

For those who have defeated cancer, I would remind you that we need to continue to live as warriors and help those who are in the middle of their own journeys by sharing our stories and advice. Celebrate those scars because they are physical proof that we could not be defeated. For those who are in the middle of their own fight, I would encourage you to reach out to those around you for support because you'll need that in those dark days and to celebrate in the small victories. Don't give up! For those who have lost loved ones to cancer, I send my love and prayers.

Syndi

HEARTWARMING

Afraid to Lose Her

Syndi Powell

ISBN-13: 978-0-373-36844-0

Afraid to Lose Her

This edition published by arrangement with Harlequin Books S.A.

For questions and comments about the quality of this book, please contact us at CustomerService@Harlequin.com.

Printed in U.S.A.

Syndi Powell started writing stories when she was young and has made it a lifelong pursuit. She's been reading Harlequin romance novels since she was in her teens and is thrilled to be on the Harlequin team. She loves to connect with readers on Twitter, @syndipowell, or on her Facebook author page, Facebook.com/syndipowellauthor.

Books by Syndi Powell

Harlequin Heartwarming

The Sweeheart Deal
Two-Part Harmony
Risk of Falling
The Reluctant Bachelor

This book is dedicated to the doctors who saved my life: Dr. Christopher Frocillo, Dr. Stephen Cahill and Dr. Salman Fateh. Thank you for your care and support through one of the most difficult times of my life. Because of your tireless dedication to your patients, many of us are able to celebrate more birthdays and holidays. We owe you so much.

CHAPTER ONE

SHERRITA LOPEZ TOOK a sip of lukewarm coffee from the cardboard cup and glanced around the group of about a dozen federal agents that had gathered in a parking lot of the building that housed the Drug Enforcement Agency. They all looked similar in navy jackets with "DEA" or "ATF" written in gold on the back. They even seemed to have the same haircut. She pulled her long brown hair over one shoulder and wished she fit in better. Maybe she shouldn't have worn her usual work outfit: navy suit jacket, white blouse and navy pants.

Her partner from Border Patrol had promised he'd meet her there, but she'd seen no sign of Desmond Jackson. A woman in a navy nylon jacket walked up to her and nodded at the cup of coffee. "That any good?"

Sherri shrugged. "It's caffeine at least."

She looked the woman over. "You with the DEA?"

"I'm Darla." The woman nodded and leaned against a parked van. "It's amazing, you know. I don't have many women in my office, but they put our agencies together and I automatically gravitate toward you. It's nice to see a feminine face among all these hard masculine ones. Like calling to like, I guess."

"It's hard being one of the few. I understand that well enough." She took another draw of her coffee. "Do you know what the scoop is with this raid? Details have been sketchy."

"Gang bringing drugs over from Canada, which is why I guess they brought you Border Patrol agents in." She glanced around. "I just wish we'd stop standing around and actually do something. But hurry up and wait seems to be the agenda for the day."

"They're probably waiting for someone. Or something."

At that, she spotted the bald head of her tall partner moving through the other agents. He stood head and shoulders above most as he wound his way around toward her. His light brown skin bathed in the early sunlight. Sherri waved Dez over and glanced at her watch. He shrugged and passed her a cup of real coffee from their favorite diner. "Had to make a stop. I know you wouldn't be able to handle the action without real coffee."

She took the cup and smiled. "Bless you."

He nodded at the female Drug Enforcement agent. "You hear anything about when we're going in?"

Sherri shook her head. "Soon, I guess."

The woman crossed her arms over her chest. "Like I said, it's the agency policy. Hurry up and wait." She held a hand out to Sherri. "Nice meeting you. How about after this we go out for lunch or something? I'd love to hear about your experience. Maybe compare notes."

Sherri shook her hand. "I'd like that. Good luck out there."

Darla nodded and walked away. Dez turned back to her. "New friend?"

"Maybe. She was happy to see another woman among all the testosterone." She finished her first coffee and searched the lot for a garbage can and walked to it and tossed it in. Turning, she took a sip of the coffee that Dez had brought her and sighed. "I hate this waiting around. Just give us our orders and let's do this thing." She turned to her partner and eyed his jeans paired with a white button-down shirt. "A little casual for you."

He looked down at his outfit. "It's a raid on a Saturday, not dinner with the president. Listen. I told the guy in charge that we'd take point, if that's okay with you."

Absolutely it was. She had jumped at the chance to volunteer in order to coordinate efforts along with Dez. She wanted to be in the middle of it. To be responsible for taking down one of the gangs bringing drugs over. This was, after all, why she'd joined Border Patrol: to guard her country from outside harm. "Sounds good to me."

One of the agents stood up in the bed of a truck and cupped his hands around his mouth to magnify the sound. Conversations stopped, and focus sharpened to the agent in charge. "Orders are being sent around now along with earpieces so we can communicate during the raid. Thank you to Agents Lopez and Jackson from Border Patrol, who will be taking point at the warehouse." He gave a nod toward them. "We'll be entering on my count. Intel says that they aren't armed and have no idea we're coming. I'd like to keep that element of surprise. Questions?"

A murmur rose, but there were no questions. A short guy wearing a bulletproof vest thrust earpieces and a receiver at them. "You're in the van."

Dez smirked as the man walked off, still handing out equipment. "He's got the body armor on, but how much you want to bet that he won't be entering the warehouse?"

Sherri adjusted the stiff vest she wore herself. She might be brave, but she wasn't stupid. As much as Dez sneered, he wore one, too. Department-issue bulletproof vest that could take a few shots, depending on the ammunition. Not that it would completely protect them if things went sideways. She glanced around the parking lot and saw several agents getting into the van. "You ready for this?"

Dez gave a short nod. "I've been waiting since six this morning to see some action."

"And you chose to leave the military why?"

"There's a difference, and you well know it." He steered her toward the van and let her get in first before following her inside. "Doesn't mean I don't miss it at times."

The drive to the riverside warehouse took about ten minutes, and they parked the vehicles in the parking lot next door to their target. Without a word, Sherri walked to the warehouse, gun in hand, scanning the docks and surrounding areas for any gang members. Empty. She reached the door that was the point of entry for the raid and stood against the wall, waiting for the signal to enter. Dez squatted behind her and leaned in close enough that she could feel his breath on her ear. "Call me crazy, but I got a bad feeling about this."

She turned and watched as one of the DEA agents counted down from five with his fingers. After he held up one finger, he waved Sherri and Dez to enter the warehouse. Sherri kicked at the door and shouted, "Federal agents! Get down! Get down!"

Chaos erupted in the warehouse. Tables overturned; guns were drawn. The noise level rose as more agents screamed out orders, and the drug dealers shouted back. Sherri wasn't certain who fired their guns first, but a barrage of bullets started to fill the air in their direction. She crouched down behind a wooden pallet and looked over at Dez, who shook his head. He pointed to his chest then to the right. Then to her and the floor.

There was no way she was going to sit still while the action happened around her. She shook her head, pointed to her chest and then to the right. Dez rolled his eyes and nodded. He pointed to himself then to her, meaning he'd follow her.

Sherri crawled to the right then stopped as she saw two shoes on the other side of the table she crouched behind. She wasn't sure if they belonged to someone on their team or to one of the drug runners, but she wasn't going to wait to find out. She pointed them out to Dez then held up her gun. She stood and held her gun out in front of her. "Federal agent. Put your hands up!"

The guy turned to face her, shooting his gun in her direction as he did so. It felt like everything was in slow motion after that. She fired her weapon twice as she fell to the floor, knocked over by the weight of Dez. She felt the back of her head smack on the concrete floor, and she moaned.

Dez looked down at her, his body lying on top of hers. "Are you okay? Did he get you?"

She squirmed under the weight of him. The sensation of his body against hers felt odd, yet familiar and intimate in the middle of a gunfight. She tucked that thought away to analyze later. "Why did you knock me down? I had him."

"More like he had you." Dez poked his head up then frowned down at her. "Stay down or you'll get us both killed."

She rolled to her belly and used her arms to push herself off the floor. "Intelligence said four or five guys and no weapons. What happened?"

"So much for the intel." He pulled her closer to his side. Bullets still flew in the air around them. He aimed his weapon at one of the drug dealers who provided suppressive fire to cover their retreat. Dez fired his gun and hit the man in the shoulder, then turned to aim at another one who shot at the DEA agents by the front door. One shot, and the man went down, too. Sherri knew Dez was a good shot. He'd been known for it in the Marine Corps, but she'd never seen it firsthand. Impressive.

"Do you plan on taking them all down one by one?"

He glanced back at her. "Right now my goal is to get us all out alive. Forget trying to subdue twenty men with a team of half that."

Sherri nodded and took in their surroundings. Two DEA agents held down one of the drug runners, but there were at least a dozen more of the bad guys by one of the exits with guns blazing. She did a perimeter check and noticed a door on the far right side of the warehouse. Probably led to an office, but it could be a means of getting out. Or there could be more of these drug runners hiding out and waiting for their time to take them all down. She pointed it out to Dez, who gave a short nod. "Go. I'll back you up."

She took a deep breath then got to her feet and ran for the office door. A man to her left turned his gun on her, and she shot him before he got the chance to put his finger on the trigger. He gave a cry and fell to the floor. She kept running, the office door ten feet away. Five. Two. One.

She tried the door handle. Locked. She hit her fist on the door then turned and shook her head at Dez. They needed to get in that room. Just like they needed to call for more backup. No one was going to get out alive if they didn't get more firepower on their side. They were outmanned and definitely outgunned.

Dez came up alongside her then pushed her away from the door. He gave the handle a kick. Nothing. Another kick, and another. On the fourth, it gave way and the door opened. Empty. Sherri entered and secured the area then nodded to Dez. He stayed in the doorway and watched for any intruders on their temporary hideout.

Sherri pressed her earpiece, trying to make sense out of the shouting and garbled nonsense. "Something's blocking our communications. You know what that means."

"No one's coming." Dez grimaced and muttered a curse word under his breath. He glanced around the office and pointed to an old rotary phone. "See if that works."

She picked up the phone and checked for a dial tone. She gave a short nod and dialed 911. After giving the address and a brief summary of events to the operator, she could feel her heart starting to slow down to a normal beat. She thanked the dispatcher and hung up the phone. "They already sent backup. Someone must have gotten word out before we lost communication."

"Good." Dez kept his gaze out on the warehouse floor, where movement seemed to have ceased. So had the gunfire. "Sounds like they've given up. Or left."

"Or they're pausing to reload."

Dez turned back, a grin splitting his face. "Always the optimist."

The sound of sirens in the background sent a wave of relief through Sherri. The cavalry was here to save them. She joined

Dez at the doorway, gun ready just in case. "We should see who's hurt."

"Feels like Fallujah all over again. I left the Corps to get away from this. That's what I don't miss about the military." He led the way back to the warehouse floor and bent down to check on a fallen woman, one of the DEA agents. He shook his head at Sherri.

She bit her lip as she leaned down and closed the woman's eyes. It was the one she'd just been joking with about being a female in a predominantly male office. They had laughed about it only an hour ago, and now she was dead and Sherri couldn't even remember the woman's name. And that seemed to hurt more.

She straightened and felt a little woozy. She shook her head, trying to clear it, and followed Dez to where more bodies lay on the floor. He took the right side of the room while she took the left. Two dead agents and five drug runners. Plus another agent and seven more bad guys wounded.

The warehouse doors opened, and four uniformed police officers swarmed inside.

Dez and Sherri holstered their weapons and held up their IDs. "Border Patrol."

One of the officers approached them and nodded. He surveyed the room. "What happened in here?"

Dez put his ID back into the pocket of his jeans. "Drug raid gone bad. I assume we have some ambulances on their way here, too."

The officer nodded. "Call came in about gunshots fired. Protocol says we get an ambo just in case." He looked Dez and Sherri up and down. "You two hurt?"

Sherri shook her head, which seemed to be buzzing. Probably the adrenaline. "We were the lucky ones."

The officer frowned and glanced at Sherri's side. "Are you sure about that?"

Sherri looked at her right side and gasped. A bullet had shredded the body armor, and a dark red stain seeped through her white blouse underneath. She put her hand over the area and found it wet. She looked over at Dez. "Did I get shot?"

Dez removed her bulletproof vest and whistled. "I'd say so, Ace." He put his arm around her. "I think we need to find a paramedic."

Sherri nodded, but it felt as if it wasn't her head that moved. Just as it wasn't her body that had been pierced by a bullet. She felt nothing. Shouldn't she feel something? She opened her mouth to say something to Dez, but blackness enveloped her.

BEFORE SHERRI COULD hit the floor, Dez scooped her up in his arms as easily as if she was a rag doll. He pushed past the officer and walked out the door of the warehouse. Too much like Fallujah. An ambulance with lights flashing waited outside in the parking lot of the warehouse. "I've got an agent down here."

A paramedic rushed to him with her medical bag. "How long has she been unconscious?"

"Not even a minute." He kneeled so that he could lay Sherri on the pavement. This was all his fault. He'd jumped at the chance to be a part of the raid and had dragged her along with him. Not that she'd protested. He had a suspicion she would have volunteered them if he hadn't first. But this was his fault. He muffled a curse word. "She didn't know she was shot."

The paramedic used scissors to cut the blouse up the side and exposed Sherri's injury. Dez knew he should probably look away, but the angry red wound drew his gaze like a moth to flame. He winced. "Is it bad?"

The paramedic shifted Sherri's body, examining it, and shook her head. "Looks like it went through but we'll take her to the hospital to be sure. She's losing a lot of blood, though." She glanced at him. "Do you know what blood type she is, by chance?"

He shook his head. He knew enough about Sherri since they'd been partners for the last four years. He knew how she liked her coffee, what she'd wear to work and how she wrinkled her nose when she laughed, but he didn't know that important detail. "Sorry."

"They'll take care of it. Don't worry." The paramedic glanced behind her at her partner. "Mark, get the stretcher. We're taking her in."

Dez grasped Sherri's hand, which lay slack in his. "I'm going with you."

The paramedic glanced at him then gave a short nod. "You sure they don't need you here anymore?"

"They'll know where to find me. She needs me more." Because there was no way he was going to leave Sherri's side now. He let go of her hand as the paramedics strapped Sherri onto the board then carried her to the ambulance. He ran behind them and jumped into the back, crouched next to Sherri as the driver slammed the doors shut, and then they were off in a flurry of lights and sirens.

Dez pushed Sherri's long hair out of her face. "She has to be okay."

"Is there anyone you can call? Her family?"

He nodded and removed his cell phone from the interior pocket of his jacket. He had her mom's number programmed in case of emergency, and there was no bigger emergency than this. He scanned through the names on his contact list then pressed Perla's name.

A hand reached out and touched his arm.

He looked up to find Sherri watching him and shaking her head. "Don't call her."

"You're hurt. She needs to know."

"I don't want her to worry." She shifted on the board and winced. "I'll call her later."

"Sorry, Ace, but this is out of your hands." He pressed the name and waited while the phone rang despite Sherri's protests. When her mom answered the other end, he gave her brief details about what had happened. "They're taking us to..."

He glanced at the paramedic who was putting an IV into Sherri's vein. "Detroit General." He repeated the information to Sherri's mom.

"How is she?" Perla asked.

Dez looked over at Sherri, who glared at him. If she didn't have one arm being poked with a needle, he was sure she'd be giving him the finger. "I think she's going to be just fine."

"Tell her I love her, and we'll be right there."

Dez hung up and gave Sherri the message. She groaned. "Just what I don't need. The waiting room filled with my family."

She winced as the paramedic packed more gauze around the bleeding wound. "My mom's going to kill me. I promised her the job was a safe one."

"It should have been. Someone tipped them off." He put a hand on Sherri's foot. "Just don't die on me. I don't want to have to get used to a new partner."

"Ha-ha." But she didn't look like she was amused. Instead, her eyes were clouded with pain that also left tight lines around her mouth.

"They'll take care of you, and you'll be back at work in no time." He said it mostly because he hoped it was true. He couldn't imagine having to work without her. Couldn't imagine living without seeing her most days. He pressed the center of his chest where there seemed to be a hot object being pushed into his skin.

The ambulance pulled into the hospital parking lot, and then the back doors were opened and people were running out to meet them. Dez stepped back as they removed Sherri from the ambulance and transferred her onto a wheeled gurney. He followed the short ER doctor as she yelled out orders to her team. "Take her to Trauma Two. And I want O neg pumped into her ASAP." She glanced up at Dez. "Anything I need to know about my patient?"

"She's a warrior. Don't let her die."

The doc gave a curt nod then ran into the ER. Dez watched her go and then dropped his head. He could stop being strong for a moment.

SHERRI WATCHED AS a team of nurses and interns buzzed around her, asking questions, removing bloody gauze, hooking her up to an IV bag, probing the wound. That last one made her sit up and shout. "Are you trying to kill me?"

The ER doctor entered the room and moved people away so that she could see the wound. Sherri looked down at the blood and swallowed back the acidic taste in her mouth. She closed her eyes and took a few deep breaths, willing herself not to pass out despite the ringing in her ears. "Is it bad?"

"I've seen worse." The doctor irrigated the wound with saline from a syringe then felt around the area with her fingertips. "Good news is that the bullet passed through, so I think you just need a few dozen stitches. My concern is the loss of blood." She probed an area above the wound and frowned. Spread her fingers out farther. "How long have you noticed this lump here, Ms. Lopez?"

Sherri looked down where the doctor had her fingers and shook her head. "I never noticed."

"Probably nothing." She turned to a nurse, giving out orders. "I'm going to suture the wound. And go check on where that blood is."

Sherri bit her lip as the doctor skillfully sewed the wound together on the front. She couldn't watch and kept her gaze on the blinds that covered the windows that looked out into the ER. "Dr. Sprader, am I going to be able to go back to work?"

The doctor didn't look up at her, but continued to place tiny stitches to bind her skin over the hole. "My guess is that a small thing like a bullet hole won't keep you down." She looked up at Sherri. "At least not for long. Now let's suture where the bullet came out."

Sherri turned on her side so the doctor could find the wound on her back. She winced as she felt fingertips trace the area. "My partner..."

"He's in the waiting room, pacing. Don't worry. I'll give him an update once I'm finished here." Dr. Sprader fell silent for a moment, the noise of the ER outside the room the only sounds. She sighed as she sutured the wound. "So how did you get a bullet in you?"

"Ambush during a drug raid." Sherri sucked in air as the wound burned.

"I'll be sure to get you some painkillers as well as antibiotics for you to take home." The doctor placed a large square of white gauze over the wound and taped it into place. "I'm also going to ask that you take it easy for a few days so that you don't rip out my handiwork too soon."

Dr. Sprader helped Sherri shift again onto her back and taped gauze over the front wound. She frowned again. "Do you mind if I check something out? I don't think it's related to your injury, but it concerns me."

Sherri nodded and watched as the doctor probed the area above the gauze on the underside of her breast. Dr. Sprader obviously didn't like what she found because she told the nurse beside her to call the radiology department to get them in for a consult. Sherri frowned. "Radiology?"

"There's a lump on the underside of your breast that I don't like." Dr. Sprader guided Sherri's fingers to the spot about the size of a half pea but hard rather than mushy. "You haven't noticed that?"

Sherri shook her head. "What do you think it is?"

"More than eighty percent of lumps are nothing, but I don't want to play around." She removed her bright pink skullcap to reveal short, spiky, dark blond hair no longer than an inch. "I've just finished my own fight with breast cancer, so I know how important it is to get answers early."

What? Cancer? Sherri tried to find words to say but couldn't seem to find any. Instead, she shook her head until the doctor put a hand on hers. "Like I said. Most turn out to be nothing, a cyst. But I'd rather be safe than sorry."

"Okay."

A nurse poked her head into the room.

"Ron says he can take her in about an hour. And she's got an army wanting to see her out in the waiting room."

Sherri closed her eyes and took another deep breath. "Mama."

"I can go get her so that she can accompany you up to radiology if you'd like."

Sherri shook her head. As comforting as the thought was of having Mama next to her while they ran tests, she had to be strong and do this on her own. "No. I don't want her to know anything yet. But I do want to see her before." She paused. "And Dez."

Dr. Sprader nodded. "I'll send her back. And she'll only know what you want to tell her."

The doctor left, and Sherri collapsed back onto the gurney. Chances are the lump Dr. Sprader had found was nothing. But what if it wasn't?

THE ER DOCTOR entered the waiting room and scanned faces until she found his. She gave a soft smile and approached where he stood among the many members of the

Lopez family. "She's asking to see you and her mother."

Dez reached around and brought Perla Lopez forward. The woman grasped the doctor's hand. "How is she?"

"She's going to be fine, Mrs. Lopez. If you follow me, I'll take you back to see her."

Dez frowned at this. "When will she be ready to go home?"

"There's some tests I'd like to run first before we release her." She wound around the various beds and rooms before taking them back to a trauma area. She opened the door and led them both inside then quietly left.

Sherri lay on the gurney, her left arm over her eyes, which she dropped to her side and held out to her mother. "I'm going to be fine, Mama."

Perla rushed to her left side and pulled her into an embrace, tears streaming from her eyes. "Desmond said that you were okay, but I needed to see it with my own eyes."

"It's okay." Sherri winced but didn't let go of her mother. "I'm okay."

Dez touched her foot still in a black boot. “They let you keep the bullet as a souvenir?”

Her eyes rose to his, and she shook her head. “No bullet. Passed right through. Just like the paramedic said.”

“She said that when you were unconscious.”

Sherri shrugged. “I heard her say it, though. I’ll have to take it easy, but other than that I’m good to go. What we need to do is figure out who tipped off our drug runners that we were coming.”

“There’s time for that later. The important part is for you to get better. How are you going to pitch your killer curveball this summer if you pull out your stitches?” He felt better talking about the coed softball team they cocaptained rather than the chance he could have lost her earlier. Easier to joke around than admit that he’d almost choked on his fear. He needed her more than he had realized, wanted her in a way he hadn’t known before. Pushing that thought aside, he leaned against one wall, his hands behind his back to avoid doing something stupid like touching her to make sure she was okay. “We’re not going to lose out to the Detroit Cop Union again. You need to be in fighting shape.”

She paled but nodded. “I will be.”

“Good.”

Perla pressed a kiss to Sherri’s forehead. “Your father, he’s been pacing the waiting room. Can I send him back?” When Sherri nodded, Perla looked up to Dez. “Would you mind going to get him?”

“Actually, Mama, I need to talk to Dez alone for a moment. Work stuff. Do you mind?”

Perla kissed Sherri again then left the room. Dez raised an eyebrow at Sherri. “You want to talk work stuff?”

“No. The doctor found something, and I don’t want Mama to know. Not yet.” She touched her chest above the white gauze that covered her wound. “A lump.”

Dez took a step forward and grasped the bed rail to keep from falling. What was she saying? “What kind of lump?”

“She doesn’t know, so that’s why she’s running more tests. Dez, I’m…” She broke off and reached out to touch his hand. “What if it’s cancer?”

He clasped her hand in his. "What if it's not?"

She swallowed, and she looked so pale. As if the blood had drained from her face and out her wound. He noticed the IV that pumped blood into her, so that couldn't be it. She brought her eyes up to his. "But what if it is? It'll change everything."

"Then we'll deal with it if it is." He squeezed her hand. "But chances are it's not. What did the doctor think?"

"Better safe than sorry. And she did say the chances are small."

He gave her a smile, hoping it showed her that he was more confident than he felt. "There you go. Stop worrying about the worst-case scenario and focus on the greater possibility that it's nothing."

Sherri let out a breath through her nose, and her nostrils flared. "Before we went into that warehouse, you remember what you said? Well, I got a bad feeling about this."

THE HOUR UNTIL she could get into her mammogram turned into two. She sent her family home with promises to call when she was released. She'd even said goodbye to Dez, who watched her with a dark emotion shining from his chocolate-brown eyes. She hated to have dumped her thoughts on him, but that was what they did. They shared everything, and this was just one more thing to add to the pile.

She'd been changed into a light pink smock that tied in the front. She could lift her right shoulder a little, but the pain from her side limited her motion. The ER doctor quickly assisted her. Sherri looked at her. "You don't have to stay with me, you know. Your job ended once I was cleaned and sutured."

Dr. Sprader didn't look at her but fastened the ties around Sherri's side to keep the smock in place. "I know, but I remember this. Waiting for tests, and then results. And all the time wondering what did I do to deserve it?" She lifted her blue-gray eyes to meet Sherri's. "I don't want you to go through it alone like I did, Ms. Lopez. Besides, I'm off duty and can do what I want."

"I'll be fine. And it's Sherri."

Dr. Sprader took a deep breath. "I'm April."

They walked out of the dressing room and into the waiting area that was painted and carpeted in various shades of pink. April gestured Sherri to a chair and grabbed a magazine. "They're running behind so we could be waiting for a while."

Sherri took the magazine and flipped through it, not able to focus on the images or words. Instead, her mind buzzed with possible outcomes. Finally, she dropped the magazine back onto the table and glanced around. Another woman in a similar pink smock gave her a tremulous smile, which Sherri tried to return, but found it too much of an effort. "When were you diagnosed?"

April looked up from her own magazine. "About a year ago. I was lucky since they found it early. But I have friends who weren't so fortunate."

"What happens next?"

"After the mammogram, a doctor will analyze the images then maybe nothing. I'll take you back to the ER, and you can go home." April touched her hand as if to reassure her this would be the result.

But Sherri was a realist, if nothing else. She could focus on what she hoped would be the outcome, but she needed to know all the facts. "And if it's not nothing?"

"An ultrasound, and maybe a biopsy. It'll be over before you know it."

Biopsy meant more needles. Sherri gave a small shudder. "And then?"

"Let's wait and see before we jump to any conclusions."

The radiology doctor must not have liked Sherri's images because she had the ultrasound and a biopsy and left the hospital with a promise that she would receive a call with results within the next few days. She called Mama to ask if one of her brothers could come pick her up and take her home.

But it was Dez who arrived in his slick dark blue sports car. He saw her standing at the entrance and got out of the car and ran to the passenger side to let her in. "What did they say?"

She shook her head. "I don't want to talk about it."

He didn't say a word, didn't ask anything, as she buckled herself into the car and waited for him to get in and drive her home. But he reached out and held her hand the entire way home.

CHAPTER TWO

SHERRI KNOCKED ON Captain White's office door and entered it when he called out her name. She handed him the typed report regarding the botched drug raid, and he started to skim it with interest. She took a seat and winced as she hit her side with the armrest. Captain White looked up at her. "You're sure you're fit to return to work?"

She'd already gotten the all clear from HR, but she nodded at her superior. "Yes, sir. It was just a twinge."

He nodded and returned to reading her report. When he finished, he looked her over. "You think they got a tip?"

"They knew we were coming, sir. Why all the firepower when previous intelligence indicated little, or none?" She shook her head. "Agent Jackson agrees with my assessment."

"Yes, he does." The captain put her report on top of Dez's and crossed his arms. "How are you really doing? If you need some time to recuperate from your injury…"

"I told you I'm fine. Sore, but nothing I can't handle." Her cell phone strapped to her belt buzzed. She saw the number and frowned. "Sorry, Captain, I need to take this. It's the hospital." She stepped out of his office and answered her phone. "Lopez here."

"Ms. Lopez, I'm Dr. VanGilder from Detroit General. I received your biopsy results, and I was hoping you could set up an appointment to come in and discuss them."

She plopped down on the edge of a nearby desk, her legs suddenly losing the ability to stay standing and upright. "So it's bad news."

There was a pause on the other end of the phone. "I'd really like to discuss this in person. Does tomorrow afternoon at four work for you?"

No. More like never worked for her. She didn't want to meet and discuss anything with this doctor. She wanted to be given a pat on the head, told she was fine then sent back into the world, whole and healthy. "Why not next week?"

"I'd rather not wait on this, Ms. Lopez."

That couldn't be good. "Then I'll make tomorrow afternoon work." She hung up her phone and looked up to see Dez watching her. She shook her head and pushed herself off the desk. Walked into the ladies' room and leaned over the sink, peering into the mirror above it. Did she look sick? Could she see the cancer that had been hiding in her body? Her eyes burned, and she closed them. Took a few deep breaths then left the restroom.

Dez waited for her in the hallway. "Bad news?"

He always knew without her telling him. Was he psychic or something? He had told her before it was more like her thoughts telegraphed onto her face, and he knew how to interpret its messages. "The doctor is going to go over the test results with me tomorrow."

Dez ducked his head and stared at the floor. He muttered a curse under his breath. "Do you want me to go with you?"

"No offense, Dez, but it's not something

I want a guy to overhear about me." She shook her head. "No, it's time that I told my mom. I should take her."

He looked up at her and put a hand on her shoulder. "If you change your mind, you know I'm here."

She was tempted to step into his arms and have him hold her until she could feel close to normal again, but didn't want to cross that line yet. She might need him later. Instead, she stepped away from Dez and walked down the hall to call her mom. "I'll be coming over tonight after work, if that's okay."

"You never have to ask for permission." Her mom paused on the other end. "I tell you what. I make your favorite enchiladas for dinner."

"You really don't need to. I wanted to see you and Dad." But she knew that telling her mom not to cook was like asking the ocean not to wave. "Thanks, Mama."

"Anytime, *mija*."

Sherri hung up the phone and walked back to her desk. Took a seat and stared at her computer monitor. She should do some work. Keep herself distracted from the thoughts in her head that threatened to pull her down into a dark place. One that she feared would spread its cold fingers around her throat and choke her.

But work had little appeal, and she ended up staring at the screen and watching the clock until she could justify leaving. She waved to Dez and left the office before he could send her any more looks of pity.

Traffic from the office to the old neighborhood distracted her enough from thinking, and she soon pulled up to her parents' house and parked on the street. She sat in the driver's seat and looked up at the home she'd lived in since she was six. Thirty years later, her parents still stayed despite offers from her and her brothers to help them move into a condo or a smaller house that wouldn't require as much upkeep. They turned them down, assuring them that they weren't that old yet. Sherri doubted that they'd ever admit when things became too much.

A rap on the passenger-side window startled her. She pressed the button for it to lower and her baby brother Hugo stuck his head inside. "Mom wants to know if you're coming in or if you plan on eating your dinner out here."

Sarcasm from her little brother? It must be a normal day in the Lopez household. "Ha-ha. I'll be right in."

Hugo peered at her, frowning. "You okay?"

She nodded and got out on the driver's side. She looked at him over the roof of her car. "Yep. How's college?"

"Don't remind me right now. Final exams next week. I've been studying so much, this is the first time I've been outdoors in the last three days."

"And graduation a week after that, don't forget." She walked around and put her left arm around his shoulders and pulled him into a hug. "We're so proud of you. Our baby is finally growing up."

She ruffled his hair, and he pushed her away. "Knock it off." He ran the rest of the short walk up to the house and opened the front door. "She's finally here. Can we eat now? I'm starving."

Mama walked into the living room and waved with her spatula to Sherri as she entered the house. "Hi, *mija*. Can you see if

Abuela is ready for dinner? She's watching her stories in her bedroom."

"Sure." Sherri walked down the hallway to the room that had once belonged to her until she'd moved out at eighteen and joined the army. She knocked softly on the door then opened it. "Abuela, dinner is ready."

"*Mi joya*, you're home." Abuela groaned as she pushed off her rocking chair and approached her. She pulled Sherri's face down to her level and gave her a loud, smacking kiss. "*Tu madre* tells me you got shot."

"It was nothing." She held up her right arm and showed off the padding under the blouse she wore. "I'll be healed in no time."

Abuela nodded then put her arm through Sherri's. "If you say it is true, it is. Now tell me more about your young man."

Sherri wanted to roll her eyes. Her grandmother never gave up on this idea that she should be married. "I don't have one, Abuela, and you know that. I'm free as a bird."

"Even birds make nests with their mates."

They slowly walked down the hall and

into the living room, where Sherri's father stared at the television screen. He muttered a curse in Spanish at the baseball players then looked up at Sherri. "Those Tigers are going to put me in an early grave."

Sherri laughed and kissed her father on his cheek. "They lose just to annoy you."

"Bah." He flipped the television off with the remote. "Let's go to the table before your *madre* chases at me with her spatula."

Dinner seemed quieter than their usual family dinners, but without her other two brothers and their families, less than half were present. Or maybe it was because Sherri stayed silent, lost in her thoughts. She looked up several times from her dinner plate to find Mama watching her, and she smiled as if to tell her that everything was okay.

After dinner Sherri volunteered to wash the dishes with Mama. Thirty years, and they still hadn't bought a dishwasher. Maybe she'd buy it as a Christmas gift and save her hands from early wrinkles. She thrust her hands into the sudsy water and pulled out a plate then swiped it with a cloth before handing it to Mama.

"Something on your mind, *mija*? I figured you wanted to talk to me when you volunteered to wash dishes."

Sherri nodded and tried to swallow the lump in her throat. Now that she was ready to tell her mother what was going on, the words got stuck and wouldn't come out. She took a deep breath and washed a glass, wiping it several times before she could turn and face her mother. "Would you come with me to the doctor tomorrow?"

Mama put the plate in the cupboard. "Of course. Are you sick?"

"I don't know." She dropped her head and let it hang while she tried to say words without turning them into sobs. "They found a lump, and they tested it, and now this doctor wants to tell me the news in person." She raised her eyes to her mother's tearful ones. "I'm scared, Mama. What if he says it's cancer? What am I gonna do?"

Mama opened her arms, and Sherri fell into them. She rubbed her back in slow circles as Sherri held on tight. "It'll be okay, *mija*. No matter what it is, you'll be fine."

Somehow with her mother saying it, Sherri felt slightly better. Maybe it would be okay.

DEZ PLACED THE cardboard cup of coffee from the diner down the street in front of Sherri, who kept her gaze on her computer monitor. “You look like hell.”

She glanced up at him then snatched the coffee. “Thanks. I couldn’t sleep last night, so I used my time to look at the drug raid from several angles.” She turned the screen so that he could see her notes. She pointed to a list. “These are the people who knew the details about the raid. One of them had to spill the beans to someone in the drug ring.”

He noted she’d put their names on the list. “Well, you can scratch us off since I know we didn’t tell anyone. Not even the captain knew the details about the raid until after it was over.”

“I’m trying to be thorough, so our names stay.” She took a long draw from the cup of coffee and sighed. “We’re missing something. I know it, but I can’t figure out what.”

"You're sure this list is inclusive? What about the DEA's informant? Where did they get their intel from?" He sipped from his own coffee and took a seat on the edge of Sherri's desk. "How do we know that their source was reliable?"

"The DEA isn't talking right now, so we're in the dark." She shook her head. "They lost agents in that raid, so they're holding their cards close to their chests." She pressed Save on the computer and pushed away from her desk. "Something doesn't seem right about this whole thing."

"You're thinking a mole?"

"I don't know yet for sure, but it does seem like someone wanted them to know we were coming. If we had kept our planned time, they probably wouldn't have been there. But then the lead agent bumped up our arrival and..."

"And they had to shoot their way out." He noticed the dark smudges under her eyes, and something inside him reared its head. He wanted desperately to protect her from whatever this was. To keep her safe. "What time is your doctor appointment?"

"Four. I came in early to make up my

shorter day. I told Mama I'd pick her up at three thirty."

She looked so small, so scared. He'd never seen her like this. She was so confident, so assured. But this same woman seemed to have shrunken into herself. He put a hand on her shoulder. "If you need anything…"

Sherri stood and crossed her arms over her chest. "Don't do that."

He looked down at himself and held his arms out. What in the world was she talking about? "I'm just offering my support."

"I'm not sick or dying." But the look on her face told a different story.

"Didn't say you were." He noticed that her eyes filled with tears, and he muttered a soft curse before pulling her in his arms. "Don't tell me this isn't appropriate, but you look like you could use a hug."

She pushed him away. "That's what I'm talking about. Don't hug me or tell me it's going to be okay. I need you to act normal. Got it?"

He sure did. His warrior was scared to death about this doctor's appointment and what it could mean for her future. Their future. A bullet had come close to taking her away from him, and now cancer could be threatening to do the same? He swallowed at the acid at the back of his throat. He couldn't lose her. His life didn't make sense without her. He nodded. "Normal. I can do that."

"Good." She picked up her coffee and looked around the office where agents started to trickle in. "Now find us a case or something to occupy our time until I have to leave."

"I've got just the thing." He pulled a file from his desk next to hers and plopped it down. "Fake IDs and passports confiscated at the Detroit-Windsor border. Want to find who's making them?"

Sherri grinned, and Dez felt like he'd gotten his partner back from her inner turmoil.

"You really know how to make this girl's day," she said.

SHERRI GLANCED AT the swarthy guy who sat in the chair across the table from her, then looked down at the file in front of her. She stood and started to pace around the interrogation room while Dez casually leaned against one wall.

He'd agreed that she'd take lead in the questioning, so she slammed a fist on the file. The guy rolled his eyes at her, which just ticked her off even more. "This is a serious matter, Giroux. You're selling fake passports and IDs, which is a felony. But then you're selling them to people on the Department of Homeland Security's watch list? Now we're talking treason." She leaned over the table. "Much more serious."

His eyes flicked to her chest. "Hey! Eyes up here, buddy. Not here." She pointed to her chest. "But here." She pointed to her face.

Dez put a hand on her arm, but she shook it off. "Giroux, you're not the mastermind behind this. We know it, you know it. So why don't you tell us who is, and maybe we can see if treason can be a mere five-year stint in prison."

Giroux eyed the door. "You got the wrong guy."

Dez picked up a box that had been sitting on the floor and dumped its contents on the table. "These look like your handiwork to me." He grabbed one and put it in front of Giroux. "This one should be familiar. We picked him up on a different charge and he gave us your name."

Giroux tossed the passport back to Dez. "You got nothing," he said and settled back in his chair as if he had all the time in the world. "But I can give you something you want."

Aha. They had him. "Now you're being smart. Who's behind the counterfeit ring?" she pressed.

Giroux shook his head. "That's small potatoes compared to what I have for you." He leaned in and dropped his voice. "You're investigating a drug raid gone bad, right? I can give you names of the guys who were there. And more important, who wasn't." Sherri tried to keep her surprise off her face, but knew she'd failed when Giroux smirked. "Yeah, you're interested."

"You don't know what I am," Sherri barked at him.

"Agent Lopez." Dez gestured toward the door. "A word?"

Sherri gave a curt nod. Once outside the interview room, she punched Dez in the shoulder. “We had him and you call me out here for a conference?”

“Because you were losing sight of what we’re here to do. And that’s to take down a bunch of counterfeiters trying to bring some scary people across our borders.”

She frowned at him. She hadn’t forgotten why they were there, but if they could get a lead on the drug raid, too? They couldn’t let that opportunity pass them by. “But what if we could do both?”

“Giroux is not going to give up both. It’s either or.” Dez paused and then added, “Come on, Sherri, we don’t want to lose this. We’ve come this far. He either gives us the ringleader on the counterfeit ring or he goes down. That’s it. No deals about the raid. No complications. Period.”

“Let me at least try. We owe it to those agents who didn’t make it. Dez, in your heart you know I’m right. And if I am, then we solve two cases at once.”

Dez waved her off. “No way. Eyes on the prize, Ace. We’re not going for extra credit here.”

“Fine. Be like that.” She opened the door and walked into the room to resume the interrogation. "Giroux, you and I both know you have no intention of doing time for your boss. Let him get the heavy sentence while you serve a couple of months in a cushy cell."

"I give you his name then I'm dead anyway."

His eyes drifted down toward her chest, and Sherri slapped the table and pointed to her eyes. Dez sat on the table on the other side of Giroux. "We can offer you protection before and during the trial, after which you'll serve a short term in a minimum security prison where you can play tennis and work on your tan."

Giroux refused. "You've got to give me something better."

Dez put his hand on the back of the chair Giroux sat in and leaned his face close to him. "There is no better, but I guarantee you that I'll give you a lot worse if you don't cooperate. The fact is, you being hauled in here has already made your boss wonder what you've told us. You really think he'll believe you didn't spill the beans?" He stood and pulled out his cell phone and threw it at Sherri, who caught it neatly.

"We're not getting anywhere. Call Spinks in the DA's office and tell him that—"

"Wait," Giroux protested. "I'll tell you."

She started to punch the number into the phone just as Dez put his hand on Giroux's shoulder. "The time for negotiation is over. You had your chance."

"No, listen!" Giroux spat and jumped up.

She glanced at Dez, who gave a short nod. She abandoned the call and handed the phone back to Dez, who pocketed it and stared at Giroux. "Sit down. We're listening."

Giroux slumped into his chair. "I'll give you his name once you put in writing that you'll protect me before and after the trial. You don't cross a guy like this without consequences."

Giroux stayed mum until they could get the Attorney General to sign off on a lesser crime with promises of protection by the US Marshal's office. Sherri took the fax with the details in with her to the interview room. She placed it on the table before Giroux and handed him a pen. "You sign, then you give us the name."

She glanced at her watch. Three o'clock

approached, and she needed to get this wrapped up so she could go pick up her mom before the doctor's appointment. Dez saw her point to her watch. "We're all good here. You go ahead and leave."

"If this wasn't important..."

"I know." Dez took the signed fax from Giroux and handed it to her. "Go give this to the cap on your way out. Giroux and I have a little business to discuss."

SHERRI PULLED INTO a parking space at the hospital and paused before turning the engine off. She looked over at Mama, who had her eyes closed, her mouth moving silently in a prayer. Sherri put a hand on her arm. "We're here."

Mama finished her prayer then opened her eyes. "I didn't tell your *padre* yet. I thought we'd wait until we had more facts."

"Thanks." Sherri got out of the car and waited for her mother. As they started walking toward the hospital, she looked up at the sky. It was a beautiful, sunny day, too nice to be getting bad news. They reached the lobby and headed to the right, where doors held signs advertising different doctors. She found Dr. VanGilder's door and opened it.

The office had a small waiting room, only four chairs and a table with magazines. A half-opened smoked glass window on one wall indicated the receptionist sat behind it. Sherri walked to the window and signed in on the clipboard then took a seat next to Mama. "You don't have to go in with me. I just need you to wait for me here, okay?"

Mama looked up at her, her brows furrowed. "Are you sure? I don't mind."

Sherri shook her head. "I have to do this on my own. But thank you for offering."

Mama picked up a magazine and started flipping through it. "I told your *padre* we'd have dinner late tonight. You're joining us."

It wasn't a question or a request. More like a demand. "I don't know if I'm going to want to eat after whatever the doctor tells me."

"You have to take care of yourself, especially now." Mama's fingers twitched. "I should have brought my knitting. Helps me think."

A nurse opened the door on the side. "Sherrita Lopez?"

Sherri stood and put a hand on Mama's shoulder then followed the nurse down a hall to an examination room. The nurse shut the door once inside then took Sherri's vitals and noted them in a file before handing her a paper vest. "Remove all clothing from the waist up. Wear the vest with the opening in the front."

Sherri took the flimsy item from the nurse and waited until she'd left the room before undressing. Once covered, she sat on the exam table and let her feet dangle. After several long minutes, a white-haired but young-looking doctor entered the room along with the nurse from earlier. He held out a hand to her. "Ms. Lopez, I'm Dr. VanGilder."

Once they shook hands, the doctor took a seat on a rolling stool and opened the file. Her file.

"I'd like to do a physical exam, then we can talk about what happens next."

He placed his hands on her body, and Sherri turned her head, focusing on the painting of a flower on the opposite wall.

She couldn't let herself think about what it was he was trying to find. The lump?

Now that she knew what it was, she'd touched the spot herself several times, checking to see if the hardness was still there. It hadn't changed. Hadn't disappeared despite her desperate hope that it would vanish and this would all be for nothing.

He checked her file, making some notes, then he looked up at her, his blue eyes full of concern from what he'd read. "I'm going to order an MRI so we can get a better picture of what's going on, but I'm afraid the news isn't good. The biopsy showed both pre-cancerous and cancer cells."

The doctor continued on about what was going to happen next, including the MRI and a lumpectomy, a less invasive and outpatient procedure. But she only heard one word out of every five. Cancer. She had cancer. She reached up and touched her breast. Inside her body, bad cells were attacking healthy ones, maybe spreading.

She could die.

She gasped, unable to get enough air into her lungs. Dr. VanGilder stopped talking and put a hand on hers. "I know this is a lot to take in, but the good news is that I think we found this early."

"How did I get it? No one in my family has had it." She'd had an aunt who'd died from breast cancer, but she'd been related by marriage, not blood.

He shrugged. "Only fifteen percent of breast cancer is found to be genetic. Everything else is environmental or lifestyle as a risk factor. The point isn't how you got it, but what we're going to do to eliminate it." He handed her a small piece of paper with instructions and details that she couldn't see, her eyes unable to focus on anything at the moment. "This is for the MRI. I have you scheduled for tomorrow morning at seven then I'll see you next Monday at nine. We'll schedule the lumpectomy for that time."

She snapped her head up. "So soon?"

"The sooner, the better, Ms. Lopez. Gives us a better chance. Do you have any other questions?"

She didn't have any because she couldn't think of anything beyond *why me?* She shook her head, feeling as if she should be more prepared. She should have done her research the night before. Found some answers before entering the office. She knew something was wrong. She could have at least looked up the disease and possible treatments on the internet.

"I'll let you get dressed, and we'll see you Monday morning." He stood and shook her hand. "I'll take good care of you, Ms. Lopez. You're not fighting this alone."

She released his hand, then sat in stunned silence. She eventually changed back into her clothes and left the exam room. The receptionist handed her a tiny card with Monday's appointment details written on it. "Have a good evening," the woman said.

Really? After hearing that news, how was she supposed to have a good anything? She opened the door to the waiting room and found Mama flipping through a pamphlet. Mama rose to her feet when she saw Sherri. "How did it go?"

Sherri glanced around at the other women waiting to see the surgeon. "We'll talk in the car."

Mama put the magazine back on the table and followed Sherri out of the hospital and to the parking lot. Sherri stood at her car, keys in her hand for a long moment as she stared at the keyhole. Mama came up and took her keys from her. "I'll drive."

Sherri nodded and walked around to the passenger side. She got in the car, fastened the seat belt and placed her purse in her lap before covering her face with her hands. Mama didn't start the car, but put an arm around her shoulder and let her cry.

DEZ PASSED THE basketball to Luke, who dribbled it several times then made a jump shot. The ball rolled around the rim of the basketball hoop then fell in. The teen pumped his fist into the air. "Yes! That's game. You owe me an ice cream."

"I know, I know." Dez used the hem of his shirt to wipe his face. He checked his watch. It was almost seven, three hours since Sherri's appointment, and he hadn't heard from her yet. Not that she'd promised to call him, but he'd hoped she would. He turned his focus onto Luke. "Did you pass that science test we talked about last week?"

The teen groaned. "Are you my mother? I thought we were just hanging out."

"I'm also your mentor and your friend who's concerned about your future. So did you pass it or not?"

Luke shrugged and bounced the ball a couple of times. "I guess. I don't know why it's such a big deal. Not like I'm going to be a doctor or nothing."

"You could be."

Luke scoffed at that and took another shot at the hoop. The ball bounced off the rim, and he ran after it to retrieve it. "Not in my neighborhood."

"Attitude like that and you won't." Dez had met Luke after he'd been arrested for shoplifting baby formula from the store across the street from the tenement he lived in. Dez's friend and family lawyer Mateo had called him in as a favor. It was the teen's first offense and the crime had been undertaken to feed his starving baby sister. The judge would let him go with a warning if he could work weekly with a mentor. Dez could identify with Luke's situation, so he'd agreed. He wiped his face again. "How many times have I got to tell you—"

"You can do whatever you set out to do." Luke rolled his eyes.

"So you have been listening to me."

"Whatever. Are we getting that ice cream or what?"

They left the basketball court and walked to the corner store. The owner eyed Luke but nodded at Dez, who went to the freezer and pulled out two sundae cones. He turned and found Luke staring at the gallons of milk in the cooler next to the freezer. He knew that look. Luke needed something, but pride kept him from speaking up. Dez took out a gallon of milk from the cooler. "I was going to pick up some groceries, too. You need anything?"

Luke turned away. "Nah, man. We're good."

Dez shifted the gallon of milk in his arms as he grabbed a couple boxes of cereal and a loaf of bread. He took his purchases up to the counter and pulled out his wallet. He turned back to Luke. "You sure you don't need anything?" Luke kept his gaze on the counter but gave a short nod. "Okay, then."

The cashier told him his total, and Dez

took out a twenty. Luke glanced away. "Diapers. The baby's out of diapers, and Mom doesn't get paid till next week."

Dez left the counter and grabbed a pack of diapers and a large canister of baby formula. He added the items to the rest of his purchases and looked at Luke again. "Anything else you need?" Luke shook his head, so Dez paid the cashier.

They left the corner store and ate their ice cream cones as they strolled back to Luke's apartment, each carrying a plastic bag. They didn't say anything until they'd reached the stairwell. Luke took a deep breath. "Thanks."

Dez put his hand on Luke's shoulder. "We talked about asking for help when you need it."

The teen still wouldn't look him in the eyes. "It's not that easy. You know what I'm talking about."

Yep, Dez sure did. He'd grown up in a series of foster homes where he learned to fight in order to get what he needed or to avoid what he didn't. That is until Ray had taken him in and taught him what it meant to be a man of honor. Not that he'd listened at first. He'd been too angry to. But the lessons had been repeated and drilled into him until he'd finally understood. "You're right. But asking for help doesn't make you weak, okay?" He handed Luke his plastic bag. "These are all for you."

Luke nodded, his eyes still down. "K."

"I'm not giving you groceries because I feel sorry for you."

Luke lifted his head, and anger and something else flashed in his gaze. Pride, maybe. "Yeah, right. You feeling guilty because you got out of a place like this? And now you got to slum it with me."

"That's not why I did it."

Luke shrugged. "Whatever, man. I gotta go."

"Next Wednesday, same time. And you'd better have aced that math test."

Luke didn't say a word, but took the bags of groceries upstairs to his apartment. At least he hadn't thrust them back on Dez. The kid must have been hungry. He wished he could remove him from this environment, because he was smart and could make something of himself if he didn't let the gangs get to him first. Or the poverty. Or the despair and hopelessness.

Dez muffled a curse and pulled out his cell phone to check again to see if Sherri had called. Nothing. He tapped out a quick message to her.

U OK?

Her response came just as quick.

Heading to the gun range. You game?

Of course he was. He texted her back in the affirmative and started his car. When he pulled into the parking lot, he noticed her car already there, plus a few others. He jogged to the front door and opened it. Smitty, the owner of the gun shop and range, gave him a nod. "Your girl is unloading a few clips in the back."

Dez raised one eyebrow at this. "That can't be good."

Smitty gave a shrug. "She seemed a little agitated, and I didn't bother to ask why."

So the doctor's appointment hadn't gone well, then. The old man looked at Dez as if he'd provide the answers, but he remained silent, not knowing what they were. Finally, Dez gave him a salute. "Semper Fi, Smitty."

He nodded. "Semper Fi."

He paid Smitty for an hour's time on the range as well as a box of bullets. In the back, he found Sherri with earmuffs and goggles on and reloading her gun with another clip. Dez walked up behind her and tapped her on the shoulder. She jumped and removed the earmuffs. "Hey," he said.

"I thought tonight was your night with Luke?"

"He already cleaned my clock on the basketball court." He studied her closely, trying to see if those were red-rimmed eyes from crying, but the goggles gave her pupils a distorted look and he couldn't gauge her mood. Instead, he turned to the target she'd been shooting at and pressed the button to bring it closer. He whistled at the holes across the target's chest. "So are you going to tell me, or can I guess from this?" He waved the target at her.

She snatched the paper from him and loaded a new one on the clip then sent it back out, this time at a distance farther away than the previous setting. She turned to him. "Doc's sending me for an MRI, so I'll be in late tomorrow."

"But what does that mean? They couldn't tell, so you need more tests?" He grabbed her hand and squeezed it. "Come on, Ace. Tell me what's going on. Don't keep me out of this." She wouldn't look at him and he swore, knowing what she wasn't saying. "It is cancer."

She nodded and threaded her fingers through his. "The appointment is a blur, and I'm sure there's things he told me that I should share with you, but I can't remember them right now. I don't know what I'm going to do."

He pulled her into his arms as she started to cry, her tears wetting his T-shirt. But he didn't care. He rubbed her back and placed a kiss on the top of her head, enjoying the feel of his arms around her. "I'll tell you what you're going to do. We're going to fight this with everything we've got."

"We?"

"You don't think I'd leave my partner to do this on her own, do you? We're doing this together. I'll drive you to appointments, and you can cry on my shoulder anytime you want." He swallowed at the emotions clogging his throat. "You're going to fight this because that's what you are. You're not a victim. You're my warrior. And that's what warriors do. They fight."

She let go of him and took a step back. "Even to the death?"

"We're not going to talk about that."

"But it could happen."

"And you could also survive this and live until you're ninety." He grasped her by her arms so she had to look him in the eyes. "You've got this. You're the strongest woman I've ever known, and something like this won't bring you down."

"I wish I had your faith," she said, clearly holding back more tears.

"So borrow mine until you find some of your own." He swore again and rubbed her shoulders. "Is there anything I can do right now?"

"Yes. Leave my cubicle so I can empty my clip onto that target." She motioned toward the hanging paper waiting for her to destroy it.

He gave a short nod. “I’ll be in the booth right next door if you need me.” He held up his gun and box of ammo. “I’ve got my own demons to shoot at.”

She smiled and put the ear protection back on. He left the cubicle and entered his own. Earmuffs in place. Gun loaded. He attached a paper target to the clip and sent it out a short distance. He aimed the gun at the center of the target and pulled the trigger, letting the kickback up his arm remind him that he was still alive. And for now, so was Sherri.

CHAPTER THREE

THE NEXT WEEK passed quickly as Sherri recuperated from the lumpectomy. She popped antacids while she waited for Dr. VanGilder to gather all the necessary information to determine what happened next. If the cancer didn't get her, Sherri figured the ulcer that must be forming in her stomach might.

She hoped that the specimen removed from her breast had clear margins indicating that all the cancer had been taken. Perhaps she'd be done with surgery and could go back to her normal life. For now, she was staying at her parents' home for the weekend. She couldn't face an empty apartment after her surgery.

Mama knocked on the open guest bedroom door and popped her head inside. "Dez is here."

Sherri groaned and propped herself up

on one elbow. "I'm not in the mood for visitors. Could you tell him I'm sleeping?"

"I won't lie to him. Not even for you. He came to see you because he's concerned about you." Mama's forehead wrinkled, and she waggled her finger at her. "You'd be so lucky to have him for a husband."

Sherri swung her legs over the side of the bed and massaged the area where the lump had been. It was still tender after three days, but the doctor had promised she'd be up and around soon. "Dez is a friend, Mama. Nothing more."

Mama didn't looked convinced. "I've seen how he watches you."

"You're imagining things. And besides, that sounds a little creepy." Mama had to be mistaken. Had to be. Dez was a friend, a good one. There wasn't anything romantic going on between them. Right? How could there be?

Mama raised one eyebrow at this, but shrugged. "He's waiting in the living room. We'll see who watches who."

Mama shut the bedroom door, and Sherri rose to her feet. She pulled on sweatpants and a zip-up jacket to cover the ratty

T-shirt she wore. She hadn't showered since the surgery—too afraid to get the sutures wet—so she probably looked like a wreck. Not that Dez would care. He'd seen her in bad shape before. Like last summer when they'd played the softball championship game that had gone into extra innings. By the time it was over, they hadn't just lost the game, she had sweat rolling down her face, her hair was damp and her softball shirt and pants were covered in dirt because she'd slid into home plate.

She opened the bedroom door and ambled down the hall to the living room, where Dez and her dad sat in matching recliners, discussing the Detroit Tigers. Conversation stopped when she entered the room, and Dez stood suddenly and motioned her to the sofa. His eyes never left hers as she walked across the room and took a seat. Dez moved to sit next to her and looked her over. "I would have come sooner, but the captain had me on an assignment and I couldn't get away. How are you?"

She tried to find the words, but unable to, she merely shrugged. Dez smiled at that and smoothed her hair away from her eyes. She backed up at his touch. He frowned and dropped his hand into his lap. “Cap can’t wait for you to come back.”

Yes, let’s focus on work rather than whatever it was that swirled around them. “There’s been developments on the raid? Tell me.”

He glanced at her dad and leaned in closer. “The ballistics report came back with interesting anomalies.”

She’d had a feeling that would be the outcome. Call it a hunch or whatever, but she’d suspected that there had been something shady going on. At least, shadier than the drug operation. “The ammo belonged to one of us, right?”

“Department-issued bullets were found on scene. And not all of them came from our guns.” He peered into her face and frowned. “Are you sure you’re well enough to talk shop?”

“I’m recuperating, not dead.” She could talk without hurting something. “What about the tests run on the drugs we found on scene?”

Dez leaned closer to her and dropped

the volume of his voice. "Consistent with what we found before. It's the same kind of dope, so the same dealers."

Sherri went and stood at the large bay window, scanning the front yard. "It's coming in right under our noses," she said. She turned back to Dez. "And they're getting help from one of *us*."

He frowned at this. "Someone with Border Patrol?"

She'd bet money that it wasn't one of their team specifically, but she couldn't rule it out. Good people did dumb things all the time. "Uh-huh. I'd stake my reputation and job on it. What's your gut telling you?"

"That we still have more questions than answers. And I don't want to make any assumptions that could cost us or set our investigation back."

She sighed. "Something else has been bothering me for the last few days. Giroux said that he knew who had been present at the raid as well as *who wasn't*. What if our inside guy didn't show up that day? Was there anyone expected to have been there who wasn't?"

Dez pulled out a small notebook and pen and made a note. "That's good. Maybe our mole wanted to be out of the way of flying bullets and passed on being there. I'll look into it." He shifted from one foot to the other. "When are you coming back to work? I'd rather we did this together."

That was the big question. She was ready for the job, tender muscles or no. She needed to be on this case, on her other cases. What she didn't need was to be sitting and doing nothing except thinking about what could be happening in her body. She craved the routine of waking up every morning and driving to the office. And part of her feared that Dr. VanGilder would find something that would take that away. That normalcy. "Tuesday afternoon I have my appointment with VanGilder. I'll have some answers after that, at least."

"Good. The office isn't the same without you."

She shook her head but smiled at this. "I've only missed a couple of days."

Dez grinned and she was struck by how it made him appear so appealing. Attractive. Handsome even. A dimple winked at her from one of his cheeks. “One day too many,” he said.

Pushing those thoughts aside—this was her partner and friend Dez after all—Sherri told him genuinely, “Thanks for coming over.”

Dez glanced around the living room and held up his hands. “Trying to get rid of me already? Your mom promised to feed me.”

Of course she did. Because that was what her mother did, stuffed everyone with food who came through the front door. Sherri wanted, no, needed, time and space to examine how confused she felt about Dez. And she'd have a clearer picture if the man himself wasn't standing in front of her looking so good.

She brought a hand up to her hair and wished she'd at least washed it in the sink. Not that her appearance had mattered when it came to Dez. Despite Mama's assertions, she knew he thought of her only in terms of friendship and work.

TUESDAY'S APPOINTMENT WITH Dr. VanGilder gave Sherri stomach cramps the more she thought about it. She dressed as if she was going to work. A cream blouse, navy jacket and pants. She tried to think of herself as putting on her armor to face whatever dragon still lay before her. If she acted like this was a typical day, then maybe that was how it would turn out.

She drove to her parents' neighborhood to pick up Mama, who had agreed to take notes while the doctor went over all the test results and made his recommendation for treatment. She pulled her car to the curb and took the tray of coffees with her to the front door. Her father answered and exclaimed when she thrust a bakery bag into his hand. "Thought you could use something sweet."

He opened the bag, then kissed Sherri's cheek. "Honey crullers. My favorite." He pushed the door open wider so that she could enter. "Your *madre* said she'd call me at work, after you talk to the surgeon, to let me know."

"I'm sorry you can't go with us."

Her dad waved his free hand. "Some stuff a father doesn't need to know."

Sherri moved ahead to the kitchen and put the tray of coffees on the counter. She took one of the paper cups and sipped from it. "It's going to be okay, Dad."

He watched her, his eyes searching hers. "Trying to convince me? Or yourself?"

She gave a half-hearted shrug. "Both maybe."

They looked at each other for a long while, but didn't say any more. Instead, her dad pulled a cruller from the bag and offered it to her. She shook her head. "I got them for you," she told him.

"Gracias."

Mama entered the kitchen, followed by Abuela. Sherri pointed to the counter. "I brought coffee and crullers, if Dad will share."

"I don't think I can eat, *mija*." Mama held a hand to her belly. "I didn't sleep at all last night and my stomach…it is in knots."

Her dad kissed Mama and hugged her tightly. "Sherri said it's going to be okay." He kissed her again. "It will be. No matter what the doctor says."

Sherri glanced at the clock on the wall. "We'd better get going just in case of rush hour."

Despite the heavy traffic, they made it to the hospital with plenty of time to spare. Sherri clasped Mama's hand in hers as they entered the doctor's office and found seats in the tiny waiting room. Mama held up a small pad and pen. "For notes, just like I promised."

Thank goodness her mom had remembered, because Sherri wasn't sure she could remember her own name at the moment. All she could focus on was the beat of her heart. Each breath took an effort, and her skin felt tight as if it would crack and break open with a simple movement.

A nurse opened the inner office door and called Sherri's name. Sherri rose to her feet and squared her shoulders. Mama nodded and stood, as well.

The next hour was spent discussing test results and the next steps. Sherri's prognosis wasn't good. Scans showed cancer peppered throughout her right breast, not just in the lump they'd removed. The biopsy indicated that it was a type of cancer that tended to spread rather than remain localized. Sherri held up her hand. "Wait. What are we talking about here?"

Dr. VanGilder looked up from the medical file and faced her. “I recommend a bilateral mastectomy.”

Sherri brought her arms up to her chest. “Both? But I thought the cancer was only in the right one.”

Dr. VanGilder stepped forward, closing the distance between them. A kind, but knowing expression on his face. “It is, although there are suspicious spots in the left I’m looking down the road.”

“And then after the surgery?”

“Depending on further test results, chemo and radiation. And once you’re healed, reconstruction.” He tried to give her a smile, but the situation didn’t seem to call for it. Instead, he let out a sigh. “When this is all over, we can give you the body you want.”

“But what if I want this one? It’s what I know.” Sherri shook her head and dropped her arms to her sides. “This isn’t fair.”

“Cancer doesn’t care about what’s fair, unfortunately.” Dr. VanGilder closed the file. “Sherri, obviously this is hard for you to take in, but the sooner we move on this, the better your chances are later.”

Mama reached out and took Sherri's hand in hers and squeezed it. "When do we do this?" Sherri asked.

He checked his tablet. "I have an opening in two weeks."

Sherri took a deep breath and let it out slowly. *So soon?* Too soon. She tried to swallow and tasted bile. What was she going to do? What was there to do but agree to the doctor's recommendation? She agreed and appreciated Mama's note-taking, since she didn't hear another word that Dr. VanGilder said after that. Her mind instead insisted she'd do what she would have to in order to survive. *Surgery?* Fine. *Chemo and radiation?* Sure. Because she wouldn't give up and give in to this disease. She would fight.

But she didn't have to be happy about it.

THIS DAY COULDN'T arrive any sooner for Dez. He'd missed seeing Sherri on a daily basis, even though he'd been with her just days ago at her parents' house. He kept watching the office door for her to enter. She'd promised to show as soon as she'd met with the surgeon. He kept his fingers crossed for good news. They could use some of that.

Noon was approaching and still no Sherri. His stomach reminded him that it needed attention. He glanced over at the office door. He could wait until Sherri arrived and then take her to lunch, so they could discuss what the doctor had said. Because her condition affected him as well as her.

She was his partner, and the job didn't work without her. Maybe she'd phone and not come in after all. He turned to check on the captain in his personal office, but Phil didn't seem to be doing anything except reviewing files and drinking coffee. She wouldn't not call Cap, but if the news wasn't great…

The office door opened and Sherri stepped forward. She looked… Angry? And maybe a little worried. He jumped up and got to her desk just as she slammed her purse down. She removed her handgun from the locked desk drawer and holstered it to her side. She winced a little, but apart from that looked the same. He watched her, waiting for her to say something. Ignoring him, she snatched the purse from the desktop and placed it in her drawer. She threw herself into the chair and looked up at him. "What?"

"I was going to ask how the appointment went, but I think I got my answer."

Sherri pursed her lips and shook her head, the loose waves of her dark brown hair falling forward around her shoulders. She kept shaking her head and refused to talk until he put a hand on her shoulder. Her eyes glistened with unshed tears. "It's going to change everything," she whispered.

That was what he'd been worried about. "What's next?"

"Double mastectomy. Chemo. Radiation. Reconstruction." She put a hand to her forehead. "I don't understand how all of this is possible. It doesn't make sense. It's as if I'm trapped in some kind of nightmare. It all feels so unreal. I'm fit and healthy. I take care of myself. I just don't get it. What did I do wrong?"

Dez was desperate to reassure her. "I don't think cancer discriminates. It can happen to anyone."

"Well, it sucks."

Dez could only nod as she stared into space, lost in her worries. He wasn't sure what else he could do for her, but he was willing to do whatever she needed. He'd sit next to her at chemo appointments. He'd bring her food when she could eat and hold her hair when she couldn't keep anything down. He only wished he could take the cancer from her. To protect her from the ravages that the treatment would inflict on her body. That was one thing he couldn't do.

Sherri rose to her feet. "I gotta go tell Cap I'll be out for six to eight weeks while I recuperate from the surgery."

Dez shot backward, almost tripping over a chair. "Six weeks without you here? No. I could barely handle a few days. You can't."

"No choice." She took a deep breath and released it, but didn't move from her spot. She seemed to focus in on him, offering him her hand. "I don't think I can do this alone, Dez. Will you come with me?"

Anything for her. "And I'm telling him that I'll be in the waiting room the day of your surgery. And any other day you need me. I'll be there for you, Sherri. I promise." He followed her into the captain's office. The click of the door shutting behind them sounded like the end of something.

WITH TWO WEEKS to go until her surgery, Sherri made a list of things she would need to accomplish before then. Cases to close. Medical supplies to purchase and store for when she'd need them.

She met with her surgeon a few days before the op, and VanGilder went over every question she and Mama could come up with, as well as a few from Dez. As she left the office with instructions for presurgery, she glimpsed Dr. Sprader sitting in the waiting room. She gave a small wave to the ER doctor. "Are you seeing Dr. VanGilder, too?"

April nodded. "He's one of the best." She put a hand on Sherri's arm. "How are you handling all this?"

"You saw my chart?"

"No, but you're walking out of a surgeon's office with a list of pre-op instructions. It doesn't take a genius to put two and two together."

"Right." She glanced at the paper and showed it to April. "It's a little overwhelming, isn't it?"

"As one who's gone through it already, I can give you some tips if you'd like."

Sherri nodded. "That would be great."

April acknowledged the nurse who had just called her name. "I should be finished here in about twenty minutes." She dug through her purse and found paper and pen, then wrote out an address. She thrust the note into Sherri's hand. "If you don't have plans tonight, we can meet for dinner. I'll tell you everything I know."

Sherri glanced down at the address and nodded. "Thanks."

"Like I said, I've been where you are right now. Maybe I can make things easier for you." April collected her things and followed the nurse out of the room.

Sherri drove to the address that April had written down and ordered an iced tea while she waited. She drummed her fingers on the wooden table and watched the entrance to the restaurant. She opened and shut the menu several times, not interested in food. She'd lost her appetite, which Mama warned her would hurt her recovery after surgery.

Maybe she could eat once the surgery was done. Because all she could think about now were knives and needles, and those took away any happy thought about enjoying a meal. She tried to ignore the images in her mind with a sip of her iced tea that the waitress had just brought over.

The door suddenly swung open and April bounced in, followed by another woman. Sherri waved them over. April pointed to the other woman. "This is Page. She's going through breast cancer treatment, too, and I thought two heads might be better than one. The more information you have, the better you'll feel."

"I'm not sure. I don't feel so great right now, to be honest."

April placed a hand on top of Sherri's. "I remember. But I promise that things will get better."

Page shook her head and adjusted the scarf around what looked to be her bald head. "Don't promise her things you can't deliver, April." Page glanced at Sherri. "April's experience with this has been far different from mine. I think that's why she invited me along. I didn't have an easy time."

April disagreed. "Hey, I didn't, either."

Page gave April a scolding look. "You breezed through it a lot more than I did."

April frowned. "I wouldn't say *breezed.* It wasn't exactly a walk in the park." She reached up and touched her short, curly hair. "But I am on the other side of it now. The better side. It's not nearly as scary. I know it sounds like your life is hitting a dead end, Sherri, but think of it as more like a detour. Your life isn't over, and Page and I are proof of that."

The waitress returned to the table, and they ordered their meals. After she left, Sherri brought out a small book and pen. "I figured I'd take notes?"

April nodded. "You'll want to write things down as much as you can. And if you can't, have someone else do it. There's a lot that's going to be thrown at you, and you don't want to miss anything."

"And if you don't understand something, ask. There's no such thing as a stupid question." Page used her straw to stir the lemon in her water. "I've been a nurse full-time for six years, but there are still things that I had to ask."

April spoke up again. "You'll be wearing tops that either button or zip up the front for the first couple of months. Nothing you have to pull over your head. Check your closet now and stock up if you need to."

"And get a bra that opens in the front." Page glanced at April. "That's what she recommended, and it was some of her best advice."

Sherri wrote every single thing down. She watched as the two women reminisced about chemo goody bags and pillows kept in their cars to protect the scars when wearing a seat belt. "I didn't realize all this stuff."

"And they're things the doctors can't tell you because most of them haven't experienced it. They can explain all about the medical supplies you'll need and things like that." April took the pad of paper from Sherri and then wrote down several more things. "But someone who has lived through it has a different perspective." She handed the book back to Sherri.

Sherri read what April had added, and smiled at the phone numbers she'd listed. "My 'in case of emergency' numbers?"

"You're going to have some bad days, and that's when you call one of us. We can talk you through it." April slipped an arm around Page. "She helped me through mine. I helped her through hers. And now we'll help you."

"Why?"

"Consider us your boob squad." At Sherri's downturned lips, April shrugged. "We'll come up with a better name. The price of membership stinks, but remember, you don't have to go through this alone. And when you're ready, you can stop in at the Hope Center. There's a lot of great resources there for women like us."

The waitress brought their salads, and conversation paused until she left the table. Page leaned in. "Have a spokesperson to give family and friends updates so you don't have to repeat the same details over and over."

April chimed in. "And let everyone who offers to help you have a chance to do something. Even if it's bringing over a pizza, or doing a load of your laundry. This isn't the time to be independent. That will come later."

Sherri stabbed a tomato, then looked from one woman to the other. "I can't tell you how much this means to me."

Page stared at her and swallowed. "Good. Because you're picking up the tab."

CHAPTER FOUR

SHERRI CHANGED INTO the soft green hospital gown and footies that the nurse gave her, then sat on the edge of the hospital bed. She clasped her hands together to keep them from shaking and tried to swallow past the lump that had lodged in her throat. In just a matter of minutes, an orderly would wheel her to the operating room and her life would be turned upside down. Was she ready for that?

A knock at the door, and the nurse ushered Dez in. He kissed Sherri lightly on the cheek. "*There* she is."

He looked hot in a baby blue T-shirt that stretched across his chest and was tucked into his worn denim jeans. She chastised herself. She shouldn't be thinking like this when she was about to have surgery. She should be focused on herself. On her body. Instead, her traitorous mind pointed out how well Dez filled out that T-shirt. And those muscled arms. They both worked out regularly to stay in shape for the job, but he looked like he'd been putting in extra time with the weights. And surely those arms would hold her tight and keep her away from harm. She sighed, stowing those thoughts away. "Did you see my parents in the waiting room?"

He nodded. "They were on their way in here, but your dad went to the gift shop for a newspaper. So I volunteered to visit you first." He leaned against the wall as if trying hard to be casual. He'd never had to try before, she noted. "Are you scared?" he asked.

Sherri wanted to reach out to him, pull him in to sit beside her, but it didn't feel right. She leaned back and rested her head on the pillow behind her. "Talk to me about work. Distract me, okay?"

Dez stepped forward and launched into the latest developments on the botched drug raid. Not that it was really news to her, but still, it felt good to have something normal to discuss. He threaded his fingers with hers and talked as if it was perfectly natural for them to be holding hands. Sherri clung to that touch and marveled at the soft skin. It should be as leathery and tough as the man next to her, but his skin felt as smooth as a baby's. He squeezed her hand, and she wanted this moment to go on forever.

Her dad poked his head into the room, and they quickly let go of each other's hand. "Hey, cupcake."

Dez tapped her on the shoulder. "I'll give you some time with your mom and dad."

He stepped out so that her parents could talk to her alone. Before he could leave, though, Sherri called out to him. "Don't go yet!"

Dez shot a look at her parents, then at her. "I'll be back before they take you." He gave a wink, then stepped outside.

Mama kissed both of her cheeks. "*Mija*, I promised to call Tia Laurie when you get out of surgery, so she can update the rest of the family. Is there anyone else you want me to call?"

Sherri motioned to the bag she'd put all her belongings in. She pulled out the notebook where April had written her phone number and Page's. "Dez said he'd call the office to let them know, but if you could call these women. They're my…support group, I guess."

Mama took the pad and put it in her purse. She kept her gaze down, and when she raised her face to Sherri's, Sherri could see unshed tears glistening in them. "Mama, we promised we wouldn't cry."

"We did. We said we'd be brave, but I don't know how right now." Two tears leaked from the corners of her eyes and made tracks down her pale cheeks.

Sherri gathered Mama into her arms and clung to her. She patted her mother's back, giving comfort to her. It was easier to do that than to face her own emotions. The nausea she was feeling was enough to deal with. She looked up at her dad, who cleared his throat. "We promised, *mi amor*."

Mama stepped back and wiped her eyes. "I know, I know."

"I'm going to be okay, Mama. Dr. Van-Gilder said this was found early, and I'm going to be just fine." She took Mama's hand and squeezed it. "More than fine. The doc's going to give me a whole new body when this is over. He already drew all over my chest with a blue marker."

"I wish this hadn't happened," her mother said under her breath.

Sherri understood that feeling. Hadn't she been thinking the same thing since she'd found out? "You have to play the cards you're dealt, and this is what I've got in my hand." She gave a shrug as if it didn't mean anything, even though it meant everything.

A nurse popped into the room and put something in Sherri's IV. The woman checked on Sherri's vitals and gave a smile to her parents. "I've given her something to relax her. Dr. VanGilder will be here soon, so it's time to say our goodbyes for now."

Mama and Daddy both kissed her, and her dad hugged her extra long. Maybe he wasn't as calm as he appeared. "We love you, *mija*," he said.

"Love you, too." As they reached the door, Sherri asked, "Can you send Dez in, please?"

Mama nodded, and then they were gone. Sherri could feel a warmth starting to spread from her arm, across her chest and down her legs. She had to lie back down so she wouldn't get dizzy and fall off the bed. She closed her eyes for a moment.

"Hey, anyone home?"

She opened one eye and saw Dez in the door frame. He took up almost the whole space. He was a fine specimen of a man. Why hadn't she ever noticed it before all of this had happened? "They're coming to get me soon, Dez. So we better make this quick."

Dez entered and stood as close to her bed as he could. With a gentle touch, he stroked her cheek. "I'll see you when you wake up."

She reached up and held his hand to her face. "You promise?"

"I'll always be here for you." He leaned down and kissed her forehead.

The warmth of his kiss combined with the drugs made her feel good and…like she was floating. "Love you, Dez."

Then she tilted her head and kissed him.

DEZ LAPPED THE waiting room for the twenty-third time and glanced at his watch for the forty-second time. How long did this surgery take? Sherri had told him it would be most of the day, but this was ridiculous. It was getting close to four in the afternoon already. He walked over to Sherri's parents. "I'm going to go get some air. Do either of you need anything from the cafeteria?"

Perla shook her head, but Horatio pulled out a twenty dollar bill. "I could use another one of the sandwiches we had earlier. The tuna?"

Dez waved the money away. "I got this." He turned back to Perla. "Are you sure I can't get you anything? Fruit? A coffee?"

She shook her head again and picked up the pace of her knitting needles, though he could tell she wasn't concentrating on her project. He'd watched her pull out stitches many times over the last six hours. "I'll be back shortly," he told them.

He found his way to the cafeteria and purchased Horatio's sandwich along with a fruit salad and a bag of chips. Not knowing how much longer they'd be here, he tried to find something to fill his time, to distract his mind from the image of Sherri strapped to a surgical table. He paid for his purchases and walked slowly to the waiting room.

And what had that kiss been about?

He'd tried not to think about that, either. Tried to put aside the feelings it had aroused in him. Not just the protective ones, since he'd always felt those. But those of a man for a woman.

He reached the elevator and pressed the up button. What had she been thinking?

Most likely, she'd been scared about what was about to happen and used the kiss as an escape. Right? She hadn't meant it. Just one friend giving another friend a kiss.

But it hadn't felt friendly. It had felt… More. As if she'd let him slip past the walls that she kept around herself. As if she'd let herself be vulnerable. With him. And that made him feel like puffing out his chest and strutting around the hospital.

She loved him. He could only hope what he felt for her mirrored that. Because what he felt was more than brotherly. Sure, he wanted to keep her safe. But he wanted to give her joy and pleasure. Wanted to feel her hand in his, her head against his shoulder.

Her lips on his.

He groaned and shook his head. She was in an operating room, fighting for her life, and he was thinking about kissing her? The elevator doors opened, and he stepped inside and pressed the button for the third floor. He needed to ignore these thoughts until Sherri was healthy and they could… What? Could he really see them dating? That wouldn't exactly fly with the captain. They'd be separated as a team, best-case scenario. Assigned to different offices or worst case, one of them would have to quit.

The doors opened to the third floor, and Dez strode down the hall toward the waiting room. The Lopezes weren't there. Dez checked around, but they had definitely left. Had something gone wrong with Sherri's surgery, and the doctor had come to retrieve them? He sat and dropped the bag of food at his feet. Maybe she was out of surgery? He willed his heart to slow down since that was most likely the case. She was safely out of surgery and her parents were talking to the doctor. He took in a deep breath and let it out slowly.

He really needed to stop imagining the worst. He blamed it on Sherri's tendency to see the glass not just half-empty, but cracked.

Horatio arrived a bit breathless and Dez went to him immediately. "She's in the recovery room, but we can't see her just yet. The surgeon said she's doing great." Horatio smiled.

Dez let out another long breath. He looked up at the ceiling, then closed his eyes. The anxiety he'd kept at bay loosened from his nerve endings and flowed out of his fingertips. She was going to be okay.

He embraced Horatio. But when he let him go and stepped back, the man was frowning. "She is going to be all right, isn't she?"

Horatio shifted where he was standing, and said, "The surgeon also told us that the cancer had spread more than the tests had shown. So she's not out of the woods yet."

"Right. But she's on the path to getting better." Dez retrieved the bag of food. "You're probably not hungry now."

"You kidding?" Horatio claimed the bag and found his sandwich, unwrapped it and took a big bite. "My little girl is fighting for her life, and she needs me to be there for her." He eyed Dez. "She needs you, too."

"I'm not going anywhere. I'll always be there for her."

Horatio nodded and took another bite.

SOMEONE GET THIS *elephant off my chest. I can't breathe.*

Sherri opened her eyes and stared at the ceiling, uncertain of where she was. She glanced down her body at the flattened chest. Oh, right. Surgery.

A nurse hurried over to her bedside and checked the readings on the electronic monitor before looking down at her. "How are we feeling?"

We? There wasn't a *we* in this situation. Sherri opened her mouth, but found that her tongue was stuck to the roof of her mouth. "Thirsty," she croaked.

"I can get you some ice chips for now. How would you rate your pain level on a scale of one to ten?"

Excruciating. Horrible. Like she couldn't take a deep breath. "Eight."

The nurse adjusted something on another machine attached to Sherri by her IV. "I'll increase this for now and get you some of the good stuff, along with that ice."

"My family?"

"They'll be able to see you in a little bit." She adjusted the blankets around Sherri. "I'll be right back."

Sherri kept staring up at the ceiling. Her arms felt too heavy to lift the blanket and look at her new body. She needed to see what now replaced what she'd known and been familiar with. Instead, she let a tear leak from one corner of her eye and trail into her hair. It wasn't supposed to be like this. She wasn't supposed to be in a hospital bed in pain with a body that had betrayed her and was now foreign. A stranger she had yet to meet.

The nurse returned and pushed a syringe into her IV. "You should be feeling better in a few minutes."

Sherri nodded and sniffled. "Sorry."

"It's okay to cry, sweetie. The anesthesia can make you emotional until it's out of your system. Plus, you've been through a major trauma." The nurse adjusted the bed so that Sherri could sit up a little and placed a cup of ice chips in her left hand.

"Chew these. And let me know if you need anything else."

Sherri clung to the cup. But what she needed couldn't be given to her by the nurse or anyone else, though the doctor had tried by removing the cancer. She needed to know that she would be healthy again after all this. That the pain would be temporary, and that she could find a new life, a better one with a new body that had conquered sickness. Maybe what she needed was patience for all of that to happen.

She took an ice chip from the cup and chewed slowly.

"LOPEZ FAMILY?"

Dez raised his head and observed the hospital aide standing in the doorway of the waiting room. Sherri's parents were already gathering their things while Dez remained seated. Perla turned to him. "Aren't you coming?"

He shook his head. "It's just for family."

Perla tugged on his arm. "You are family."

Dez was taken aback at the sudden swell of emotion that he felt. *Family.* Something he hadn't had in a very long time. Yet the Lopezes had come close in the last few years. Inviting him to barbecues and to celebrate the holidays. Feeding him until he couldn't move. Perla had even knitted him a navy blue scarf that was still his favorite. He rose to his feet and followed them down the hall, like part of the family.

The aide led them to a big room where a dozen beds hid behind thin individual light green curtains. The aide pushed one curtain back, then left them. Dez paused, unsure of what he'd find lying in the bed. He hung back, allowing Sherri's parents to surround her.

Perla finger-combed Sherri's hair and kissed her forehead. She spoke her name tenderly and reverently, as if a prayer.

Horatio gripped the bed rails and didn't say a word. Dez knew what he felt. The woman in the hospital bed resembled Sherri, but it was a version of her that Dez found frightening. Not the warrior he'd always recognized, but a scarred and emotional weakling who winced with pain and spoke so softly she could barely be heard.

It wasn't fair. Dez wanted to punch

something because Sherri didn't deserve this. He clenched his hands into tight fists. If she couldn't fight, then he would.

He stepped inside the curtained area and smiled at her. "Some people will use any excuse to get out of softball practice."

Her eyes crinkled slightly, and she gave a thin smile. That was his Sherri. She was still in there. "I'm afraid you'll have to lead the team by yourself this year."

"I don't think so. There's no reason that you can't yell orders from the bench." He tilted his head to the side. "Wait a minute. That sounds like what you always did anyway."

"Funny." Sherri shifted, trying to sit up higher, but then closed her eyes and groaned, as her breaths came out hard and heavy.

Perla put a hand on Sherri's. "What is it, *mija*? Do you need something?"

"It hurts."

He bet it did. "I can get the nurse," he offered.

Sherri frowned. "I can't have any more pain medication for another two hours." She looked over at her mom. "Should it hurt this much so soon?" She gripped her mom's hand. "I didn't think it would be like this."

"I'm sure it will get better." Perla patted her hand. "It has to, right?"

Sherri burrowed under the blankets. The curtain was swept aside and a nurse gave them a cursory glance before focusing on Sherri. "How's the pain from one to ten?"

Sherri moaned. "Still an eight. Why hasn't it changed?"

The nurse hustled Perla out of the way so she could check the IV drip and adjusted the speed of the clear liquid running into Sherri's arm. "They've assigned your room, so we'll be moving you in about twenty minutes. I'll make sure to tell your floor nurse about your pain levels." She looked at the Lopezes. "I can give you the room number if you'd like to go out for dinner and return once she's in her own room."

Dez didn't want to leave Sherri's side. He wanted to be there for her at a moment's notice. He didn't need food. He only needed her. He stepped closer to the hospital bed. "You two go on ahead. I'll stay with her."

Perla glanced at Horatio, then Sherri.

"Do you want us to leave? Horry, I think we should wait, don't you? What if she needs something?"

"Go, Mama. You don't have to worry. Dez will take care of me."

Perla gave a short nod then tucked her hand in Horatio's before leaving the recovery ward. Dez got a chair and sat at the end of Sherri's bed. He put a hand on her blanket-covered foot. "Do you need anything?"

Sherri's face crumpled, and she broke down in tears. "Oh, Dez. It wasn't supposed to be like this."

"And how do you know what it was supposed to be like? You've never been through it."

"They didn't tell me the pain would be *this* bad. They said the anesthesia would help keep the pain down the first night, but it feels like a ton of bricks crushing my chest. I don't know if I can do this."

He frowned at her. Who had suddenly inhabited and taken over his best friend? "Now, you listen to me, Sherrita Maria Consuelo Lopez. You are a strong, independent woman who can do anything that she sets her mind to. *So you decide right now.* Are you going to stay this victim who lets things happen to her or are you going to be that warrior who makes things happen?"

She wiped at the tears that still fell down her face. "You don't understand."

"I do understand a lot better than you realize. I watched my foster father wither away from the chemo and radiation and all the drug trials that the doctors put him through. But the thing is, he'd given up as soon as he learned it was cancer." Dez got up and moved in close, staring down at her. Then he kneeled beside her so they could be at eye level. "Are you giving up? Or are you going to fight this pain? Will you succumb to it and let weakness in, or will you use it to get stronger? To build yourself back up?"

Sherri stared at him hard. "I really hate you right now."

"Good."

He bristled until she broke into a smile. "You're the only one I would let talk to me like that."

He answered her grin and reached out to

cup her cheek. "I'm tough on you because I know you can take it. You're no crybaby."

Her smile faltered, and she reached up to touch his hand. "I'm not quite in any condition to fight just yet."

He smiled more. "That's okay. I'll get you there."

LATER, SHE WOKE to find Dez asleep in a chair next to her hospital bed, holding her hand. She watched him. So strong. And so determined to make her whole again. She worried that the whole he envisioned was different from her new reality.

She'd lost parts of herself in the surgery. She'd always been known for her big chest. Been admired for it. And now, glancing down at the soft mounds underneath the gauze, she would never get that back.

It was a small thing, really, but at that moment it felt important.

The door opened and Sherri dropped Dez's hand as the night nurse swept into the room. The nurse kept his gaze on Sherri. "Pain any better? Keri said you were having a hard time getting ahead of it when you first got here."

"It's not as intense, but it's still there."

"Unfortunately, it's going to be like that for a while." He checked the bedside table. "My name is Justin, and I'll be taking care of you tonight. Is there anything I can get you? Something to eat or drink? An extra pillow?"

She glanced down at the beige hose with a red button at the end. "I'm okay for now, but I use this to summon you?"

Justin laughed at that. "Summon, huh? You're going to be one of *those* patients?"

"Hardly."

Justin wrapped the hose around the bed rail so that it wouldn't fall or get trapped underneath her. "Yes, you can summon me with that button, but please only use it if you have to. You're one of twenty patients that I'm caring for tonight." He adjusted her pillows behind her. "I'll come back in an hour with your next pain injection."

Dez stirred and stretched on the chair. She switched her attention from Justin to Dez. "Hey, you should go home. It's been a long day."

"You heard the man. You're one of

twenty patients. I've got arms and legs you can use to get whatever you want."

She narrowed her eyes at him. "I want to go home. Can you do that?"

"Nice try." He stood and stretched some more before taking a short walk around the room, pausing to bend every few steps. "Have you gotten out of that bed at all? Maybe we could get you up and walking down the hallway for a bit."

The thought of trying to use her body made her nauseated. She shook her head. "No. Later."

April's voice preceded her. "Actually, your partner makes a good point. The sooner you get mobile, the sooner you can get out of here." April swept into the room and immediately adjusted the height of the hospital bed so that it was lower to the floor. "Let's give it a try."

Sherri scowled at her. Who did she think she was? She might be a doctor, but she wasn't assigned to Sherri. "You come to visit, or to torture me? I just got out of surgery."

"Perfect time to get up and at 'em." She glanced over at Dez. "Agent Hottie, you going to stand there, or help me get Sherri to her feet?"

Dez hesitated, but then walked promptly to the side of the bed. April moved the IV stand so that it stood closer to Sherri. She checked the tubes, then held out a hand to Sherri. "I can give you a boost, but it will hurt less if you do this yourself."

Sherri made a face at April. The woman didn't seem to be joking about her getting out of the hospital bed. "I didn't ask you to come here."

"No, you asked for my support. Well, this is it." She encouraged Sherri to stand. "Listen, I wish I'd gotten up sooner after my surgery. I know what I'm talking about."

She couldn't get out of this, could she? Sherri scooted to the side of the bed, then moaned as she pulled herself to a sitting position. It felt as if lightning bolts had shot through her armpits. Taking a few deep breaths, she swung her legs over the side of the bed, then placed her feet on the floor. A countdown from ten, then she pushed off the bed. April grasped one arm as Dez took the other, steadying her.

"You're doing good so far." April nodded vigorously. "Let's just make it to the door the first time."

Sherri put one hand on the IV stand and took a step. It hurt to breathe as if she was stuck in a vise. Another step. She swallowed at the bile at the back of her throat. "I feel like a baby learning how to walk."

"It's not as bad as all that. It's not like you had knee surgery." April stood back so that Sherri could pass by her as she edged toward the door. "You're almost there."

Sherri calculated the amount of space between her and the door. Six feet, maybe seven. "I can do this."

"Yes, you can," Dez said behind her. "We never doubted it."

But she had. At the mere mention of getting out of bed, she thought she would never be able to make it. Yet here she was. Standing on the threshold, looking out into the hallway of the hospital wing. She glanced behind her. "Think I can walk to the nurses' station?"

April smiled. "Fantastic idea."

"While you ladies take a stroll, I'm going to check in with the office and find the restroom." Dez put a hand on Sherri's shoulder. "That's my fighter."

April watched him leave, then turned to Sherri. "What is the deal between the two of you? Just work partners?"

"Best friends." And maybe something more. How many of her friends had spent the entire day in a waiting room, then slept in a chair beside her bed in case she needed something? "I don't know what I'd do without him."

They fell silent as Sherri focused on each step. Once they reached the nurses' station, she gave a wave to Justin, then turned and started the slow journey back to her room. It took only minutes, but felt like hours. Finally, April helped Sherri get back into bed and made sure she wasn't lying on an IV tube. Sherri tried to use her arms, but found them stiff.

"The surgeon cut through your chest muscle, so you'll need some physical therapy to get back your range of motion. Do things like walking your fingers up the wall. Letting your arm dangle and moving it in circles. They'll go over all that with you before they send you home." April took the seat that Dez had vacated. She adjusted the pillow behind her back, then turned to Sherri. "So have you looked yet?"

Sherri glanced down at the gauze and bandages that covered her chest. "No."

"It's not as scary as you think. Right now everything is red and swollen. But that will go away." April shrugged. "Some women never look, much less touch. But it's part of your body now. It's okay."

"I checked those websites you told me about. The ones with the pictures of post-mastectomy women, so that I'd be prepared for what I'd see. But now that it's time, I don't know if I can." Sherri pulled the edge of the sheet up to her chin. "Maybe later."

Dez entered the room, followed by Sherri's parents. "Look who I found wandering the halls."

April put an arm on Sherri's shoulder. "I'll get out of your hair for now. Page said she'd stop by during her break later tonight. Believe it or not, you're looking good and on your way to recovering. Don't get discouraged." She gave her a quick, light hug then waved to Sherri's family before leaving.

Sherri didn't feel so good, though. Her mom set two plastic containers on the bedside table. "We had dinner at that Italian place you like, and Giuseppe made your favorite."

The thought of lobster ravioli didn't make her stomach growl with anticipation like it usually did. Another change to her life or a temporary side effect of coming down from the anesthesia? Sherri wasn't sure which.

Mama held out a container and plastic silverware and napkin to Dez. "He knew your favorite, too."

Dez rubbed his hands together. "You do know your way to my heart." He opened the lid and took an appreciative sniff. "Chicken scallopini."

Her dad held up a white paper bag. "And extra garlic bread."

Her mom passed her the container with her dinner. "You need to eat, Sherri. You haven't had anything since last night."

She winced at the bitter taste in her mouth. "I'm not hungry."

"I can feed you like when you were a baby, or you can be a big girl and eat one bite." Her mom placed a half ravioli on a plastic fork and held it up to Sherri's mouth. "You won't heal if you don't eat right."

Sherri opened her mouth and took a small bite. She chewed it slowly, then swallowed. "Fine." She took the container and the fork and started feeding herself. Mama smiled. Things were now back to normal, at least in Mama's world.

DEZ TRIED TO get comfortable in the chair next to Sherri's bed, careful to not make any noise and wake her. The dark circles under her eyes worried him, but he knew they were only temporary. Once she got some rest, she'd be okay.

The door to the room opened, and the nurse came in to check on Sherri like he had every two hours throughout the night. He checked her vitals and the levels on her IV before pressing on her shoulder. "Medication time."

She yawned and accepted the tiny cup of pills. She shot the meds back, then sipped some water. "What time is it?"

"Two." Justin checked her bandages and her drains. "Your surgeon will be in about the same time as your next pain meds." He secured the straps of the compression bra and pulled the sheet over Sherri's shoulders.

"So early?"

"VanGilder likes to get an early start." Justin took the empty paper cup "I'll get you more water. Is there anything else you need?" When Sherri indicated there wasn't, he turned to Dez. "Sir?"

"I'm fine."

Sherri turned to glare at him. "You should go home."

Dez shook his head as Justin left the room. "I'm not leaving. I promised your parents I would stay with you."

"I'm not a baby."

"I want to help you, so don't make me leave." Dez reached over and pushed a strand of her brown hair back behind her ear. "There's not much I can do, but I can do this. I can be here for you."

"But you won't get much sleep in that chair."

"Like you're doing any better in that bed?" Dez gave a soft laugh, then leaned over her to switch off the light above her head. “Let’s try and get some sleep. That is, if you don’t start snoring again.”

“I don’t snore.”

He chuckled at that and settled in the chair, pushing out the leg rest so that it would recline at a slight angle. He crossed his arms over his chest and closed his eyes.

“Dez?” Her voice was a whisper in the darkness. “Thank you.”

He smiled and nestled into the chair. “You’re welcome.”

He wished that he could do more. He would take the cancer himself, if it meant that she would be healed and whole. There was nothing he wanted more. Unless it was to be a part of her life. She’d said she loved him, but she offered nothing to go with the words. And he would want to have more than words. He wanted her, heart and soul.

CHAPTER FIVE

THE THIRD DAY after the operation, the surgeon released her from the hospital. The drive home hurt, as every bump in the road jostled her and caused prickles of pain to make her cranky. Then there were the stairs to her apartment. She normally eschewed the elevator in order to get more exercise, but she could only walk up three steps before conceding defeat.

Mama followed her, carrying various bags holding the flotsam that would be her world for the next week. Once Mama unlocked the apartment door, Sherri paused before entering. Should she go to the sofa, which was closer, or directly to the bedroom where she'd be more comfortable?

"Are you going to stand out here all night?"

Sherri turned, slowly, cautiously, to see

Dez carrying more bags. "What are you doing here?"

"I promised your mother that I'd pick up some groceries. I know how you like to keep your fridge." He winked at her. "Empty."

"I have orange juice," she argued.

"I stand corrected." He shifted his weight and adjusted the bags of food. "Now, are we going inside, or what?"

"I'm trying to decide where to rest." She took a few steps so that she was actually inside the apartment. "I want to take some pain pills and then a nap."

Mama held out her hands to Dez. "You are a good boy." She kissed his cheeks loudly, then took the bags from him. "If Sherri was smart, she'd snap you up before someone else did."

Sherri groaned. "I told you, Mama, we're friends."

Dez nodded. "Best friends."

Sherri smiled at him. "The best." She took a few more steps, then clasped the back of a dining room chair. "I need to lie down."

"Sofa or bed?"

Sherri looked at the sofa, then shrugged. "Bed."

Dez swung her up in his arms, and she grimaced as the prickles of pain made themselves known again. But then he carried her to her bedroom as tenderly as he would a newborn. He gently laid her on the bed, then held up a finger. "Be right back."

Sherri pulled the comforter aside and dragged it over her, shoes and all. Dez returned a moment later with two white pills and a large glass of water. "Here."

She accepted the pills, but her hand shook as she took several gulps of water from the glass. It dribbled down the sides of her mouth and onto her bright orange hoodie. She gave the empty glass back to Dez. "Thank you."

"Do you need anything else?"

She shook her head. "Just sleep." She snuggled farther under the covers and closed her eyes. She registered lips on her forehead and then the removal of her shoes before she succumbed to the fatigue that had been following on her heels ever since the hospital.

DEZ SPENT THE weekend checking up on Sherri and returned to work on Monday fearing the sight of her empty desk. While he appreciated that she was on the mend, it was going to be a while before she was back in fighting form.

He entered the office, carefully balancing his cup of coffee. He collapsed into his desk chair and shifted it to avoid seeing Sherri's vacant desk.

The captain's office door opened. "Jackson. Now."

Dez rose to his feet and practically snapped to attention. He hightailed it to the captain's office and stopped short at the sight of his friend sitting in front of Cap's desk. "Ras?"

Miles Rasczynski stood up and slapped hands with Dez before bringing him into a chest bump. "Dez, it's been a long time."

"Last I heard you're with Homeland Security. What happened to the Corps owning you body and soul?" Ras and Dez had been stationed together with the Marine Corps in Afghanistan. They'd seen some action, which had made them as close as brothers.

Ras lifted his pant leg to reveal a titanium prosthetic. "Left a part of me in Kabul and the Corps retired me. So I figured protecting our borders at home would be just as important."

"If you two are finished flapping your jaws, maybe we can sit down and discuss the business at hand." Cap took a seat behind his desk. Dez and Ras sat, as well. "Rasczynski has been assigned to our office on a temporary basis, so I figured with Lopez out, I'd partner the two of you up." Cap handed a file folder to Ras. "Here are copies of the reports on the open cases they've been working on. And I'm sure that Jackson could use some fresh insights into the drug raid fiasco." Cap stood and glared down at them. "I expect results, gentlemen, not excuses. Go get me some answers."

Dez jumped up, and Ras followed him out of the office. Ras said, "The captain reminds me of some of our drill sergeants that we had on Parris Island."

"Cap would put those dudes to shame." Dez motioned to Sherri's desk. "Use this, but don't get too comfortable. My partner is coming back for it."

Ras put the folder on the desk. "The captain mentioned that she's out on medical leave."

Dez didn't offer any more details. Ras may be like a brother, but some things needed to be kept close to the chest. "She'll get better."

"You ever miss the Corps?"

"Sometimes. But I like not getting shot at or blown up even more." Dez picked up his coffee and took a long sip. "That's why this drug raid gone bad has me on edge. The crew had a reputation for running without guns, but we show up to the warehouse and suddenly they're armed to the teeth. Doesn't make sense unless they got the heads-up we were coming."

"You have an idea who told them?"

Dez shook his head. "DEA says they've checked and cleared all their agents, but I have my doubts. Because if it wasn't one of them, it was one of us. And that's not something I'm willing to accept right now."

Ras flipped open the file and thumbed through a few pages. "Why don't I read over these notes, then we can strategize our next step over lunch? You can walk me through what happened, blow by blow."

"You bet." Dez booted up his computer while Ras took a seat at Sherri's desk. Dez pulled out his cell phone and tapped a quick message to Sherri, asking how she was feeling.

Her response was immediate.

Okay. I miss the office already.

He smiled at that. She missed him, even if the message didn't include those words. Dez texted back.

Got a new partner.

So soon?

Guy I knew from the marines. You'd like him.

Doubt it.

Dez grinned and ran a hand over his face. He had it bad for Sherri, thinking of how she could light up a room just by being in it. He needed to keep an edge, a distance. Otherwise he would lose not just his professionalism, but also his focus on a job that required it 24/7. That was why the department discouraged dating between partners. More than discouraged, they transferred one of the parties out. And that was something Dez would avoid at all costs. He didn't want to change what they had.

But then there was a small part of him that wondered what if their relationship did change.

Get some rest so you can get your butt back here soon.

He put his phone back into his pocket and concentrated on the file in front of him.

DEZ PICKED UP a pizza and drove over to Sherri's apartment. He heard loud voices on the other side of the door when he lifted his hand to knock. He used the doorbell in case they were yelling too loud to hear him.

Perla opened the door and stared at him. "Good. I need backup." She pulled him inside where Sherri stood at the kitchen counter, grasping the edge. Perla pointed at her. “You tell her to do what she has to do.”

Dez frowned and looked from Sherri to Perla and back again. “What isn’t she doing?”

“It’s nothing.” Sherri glared at her mother. “Less than nothing.” She pulled the sleeves of the orange hoodie down over her fingers.

He waited for one of them to share more details, but they were intent on staring each other down. He held up the pizza box. “I brought dinner.”

“Mama cooked.”

He only just then noticed the aroma of spicy beef in the air. “Well, lunch tomorrow, then.” He waited some more and said to Sherri, “So? Tell me what’s going on.”

Sherri rolled her eyes. “She wants me to take a shower.”

That didn’t sound so horrible. “And the problem is…”

Perla huffed. “She can’t lift her arms enough to wash herself. So I volunteered to help her, but she’s too proud to accept.”

Sherri disagreed. “It’s not that.”

“Then what is it?” Dez asked.

"I'm not a baby who needs her mommy to bathe her." Sherri covered her face. "I hate this. I hate that I have to depend on someone else." She removed her hands and looked up at Dez. "This is wrong."

"Yes, it is," he told her.

He took a step toward her, but she retreated two and closed her eyes. "When am I going to feel normal again? When is any of this going back to what it was before? Because right now it feels like never. And that's too long."

This time, Dez crossed the room in three long strides and took her into his arms. She leaned against him, but didn't put her arms around him. He rubbed her back and swayed back and forth, trying to soothe her somehow. Not that it would make up for what had already been taken from her.

"One day you'll look back on this and realize that things did get better. That what you're feeling will eventually go away." He kissed the top of her head. "I promise it will get better."

He looked at Perla. She gave a soft nod and mouthed, "Thank you."

"Fine." Sherri took a step back from Dez. "Let's go take that shower, Mama."

LATER, SHERRI WALKED out of the bathroom with wet hair and in the same bright orange hoodie, but clean sweatpants. Dez turned from the baseball game he'd been watching and whistled. She shot him a dirty look. He shrugged and patted the sofa beside him. "How do you feel?"

"Better. Tired." She sat next to him and leaned her head on his shoulder. "So tired."

"Go ahead. Take a nap." He turned down the volume of the television. "I'll wake you up when I leave."

Her eyes drifted closed, and he leaned down to check on her.

Perla returned to the living room and saw Sherri sleeping on his shoulder. She gave a soft smile and walked into the kitchen. She returned moments later with a plate of beef enchiladas and a fork. She balanced it on the sofa arm by his free side, then kissed his cheek. "She doesn't know what a good man she has in you."

Dez glanced at Sherri, then focused on

his food. "We're best friends. I'd hate to change what we have."

"And you don't want more?"

He avoided the question and took a bite of enchilada. "This is so good. You're the best cook I know."

"Mmm-hmm." She eyed him but didn't push the issue. Instead, she left the living room to return with her own plate. She sat in the gliding rocker and they ate in silence for a while.

He glanced at Sherri again, who snored softly and rubbed her face into his shoulder. "How is she really doing?"

Perla gave a shrug and put her fork down on her empty plate. "She's so..." She shook her head. "Angry."

"I guess that's understandable."

"But anger isn't going to help her get better."

"But it might motivate her to do more things for herself. To push herself." He'd seen her do it in the past. When they had lost an agent in their office to a senseless shooting, he'd watched her as she pursued the leads to find the shooter and make sure justice was served. She'd pushed herself on the baseball field when they had faced their rivals, the Detroit Cop Union. He'd seen her working out when she was determined to be in better shape after a less than satisfactory job rating.

She didn't give up. She used her emotions to become better. She'd done it before, and she'd do it this time, too.

"I guess." Perla sighed and placed her plate on the coffee table. "I wish I could take all of this from her and do it myself. I don't like seeing my daughter go through this."

They had that in common. "I don't, either. But she's tough, and that's got to mean something."

Perla stood and took his empty plate from him and picked hers up from the coffee table. "I'm sorry I don't have anything for dessert. Sherri might have some ice cream, though."

"I'm fine, Mrs. Lopez." He loosened his arm around Sherri. "And thank you for dinner."

She gave him a sad smile. "I can't cure cancer, but I can cook."

SHERRI WOKE TO a darkened bedroom. She looked around, wondering how she had gotten there. The last thing she knew, she'd been sleeping on Dez's shoulder while they watched a baseball game.

He must have put her to bed. The thought made her squirm. Had she picked up her laundry? Or made her bed that morning? She hadn't been doing much of anything lately, and if Dez had seen her unmentionables, she wasn't sure how to face him the next time he came over.

Sherri lay on her back, staring at the ceiling. She'd always been a side sleeper, but the first night home she had tried to sleep that way and the pain had been unbearable. Now she had to sleep on her back. Just another change in her messed-up life.

What time was it? She squinted at the alarm clock. After three. She'd been sleeping for almost seven hours. Now that she was wide awake, she tried to sit up without using her arms to brace herself; another thing she'd had to adjust to. Once upright, she swung her legs to the side of the bed and pushed up onto her feet. She walked to the bedroom door, opened it, then poked her head out. Everything was dark.

Letting her eyes adjust to the dark before walking down the hall, she noted that the door to the guest room where Mama slept was open. Probably so she could hear Sherri if she needed her mom in the middle of the night. Sherri gave a soft smile. In the living room, she turned the television on, muting the sound while she flipped through the channels. Not that she wanted to watch anything, but she needed some kind of distraction.

She hated what her life had become. Hated having to depend on someone else to do the most mundane things like wash her hair or get a glass from the cupboard. Page and April had tried to tell her what to expect, but they'd also warned her that she would have to go through things that even they couldn't warn her about. That she'd have experiences that were uniquely hers. It made her feel even more alone.

She flipped through more channels and found some *I Love Lucy* reruns. She hadn't watched the show since she was a girl and Mama had gotten the video set for Christmas. She settled into the couch and turned the volume up a tad, but still low enough that it wouldn't disturb her mom.

One show ran into another, and by the time her mom woke up to make breakfast at six, Sherri had watched enough episodes to make her feel as if her eyeballs would shrivel to dust. Mama put a hand on her forehead. "What time did you get up?"

Sherri yawned and stretched. "Three. I couldn't sleep."

"Why didn't you wake me?"

"Because you needed your sleep."

Mama went into the kitchen as Sherri slowly stood up and waited a moment before trying to follow her. She found her mom taking eggs out of the fridge. "I appreciate all you're doing for me, but I should start taking care of myself."

Mama shook her head. "It's too soon. You couldn't even take a shower on your own yesterday."

And that made this all the harder. "No, I need to push myself more."

Her mom stopped cracking eggs into a bowl and started to whisk them. "Don't push yourself so hard that you hurt yourself."

"I won't. I know my limitations." Her mom gave her that look only mothers knew until Sherri smiled wryly. "Well, at least I'll figure out what they are soon enough."

"You're trying to get rid of me already?"

"Dad needs you, too. And Hugo." She swallowed and kept her gaze on the white tile counter. "I have to be able to do this on my own."

"But you don't need to."

Sherri looked up at her. "Yes, I do."

Mama stepped away from her to pour the eggs into the hot skillet on the stove. She seasoned them and took two plates from a cupboard. For a while, Mama cooked while Sherri walked her fingers up the wall next to the front door. She made it about an inch higher than she had the day before and counted it as a victory.

Mama plated the eggs then placed them on the dining room table. Sherri took a seat in front of her plate. Before they ate, Sherri put her arm on the table and held out her hand to her mom. "Thank you."

"It's just eggs."

"It's more than that, and you know it." Sherri squeezed her mom's hand, then let it go.

THE FIRST WEEK without Sherri at work passed slowly, slower than Dez would have liked. On Wednesday he met up with Luke at the basketball court, but thoughts of Sherri distracted him, and he lost the first game. Luke glared at him. "Are you trying to take it easy on me?"

Dez shook his head. "Got my mind on something else."

Luke eyed him. "A girl?"

"Yes, a woman, actually." Dez dribbled the ball then passed it to Luke. "You know my partner, Sherri? She's got cancer."

Luke winced. "She gonna die?"

"Not if I can help it." Dez charged him and stole the ball, then he turned to make a perfect hook shot into the basket. "Two, zip." He bounced the ball to Luke. "Let's see what you got."

They played two more games before sitting on the sidelines, the backs of their T-shirts drenched with sweat. Dez took his shirt off and wiped his face. He stared out across the court. "How'd you do on that math test?"

"Passed, of course." Luke flipped the basketball in his hands. "The counselor told me yesterday that I brought my grades up enough that I'll graduate in June."

Dez punched him in the shoulder. "And you waited until now to tell me? That's great news, man."

"Thanks to my tutor." Luke punched him back. "And you."

"I didn't do anything. Just played some basketball."

"And encouraged me to keep trying. Which is more than what my dad ever did." Luke got to his feet and looked toward the horizon where the sun hadn't yet set. "He's never even laid eyes on me, you know? Left my mom before I was born, like I didn't matter to him."

Dez kept quiet, knowing Luke needed to let this out. He could understand where the kid was coming from. Hadn't he been in that same boat? Never knew his dad. Mom had loved drugs more than him. And he'd ended up in the foster care system by the time he was five. Moved from place to place. Seeking out somewhere that he could belong. Gangs in his neighborhood had been attractive because at least he could belong to something, to someone. He could have ended up in a different place than where he was if it hadn't been for Ray, who insisted he toe the line and quit the gang. His foster father had shown him right from wrong. That family stood up for each other. That life meant being responsible for yourself and those you loved. Dez missed that man every day.

And now he had Sherri, who had become his family. He couldn't lose her. Not to cancer or the job or anything else. She, above everything, gave him purpose. It was his goal to be a man whom she could be proud of. He closed his eyes and sent positive thoughts in her direction.

Luke cleared his throat and stood. "I won two games, which means you owe me an ice cream."

Dez groaned as he got off the ground and put his shirt back on. "You're on."

As they walked to the corner store, Luke glanced at Dez. "Sorry about your friend."

"Thanks."

On Friday, Dez sped out of the parking lot from work and headed directly to Sherri's apartment. He hadn't seen her since Monday, and he needed to be around her again. He took the stairs two at a time and knocked on the apartment door.

Horatio answered the knock. "Desmond, she's been asking for you."

"Sherri?"

He shook his head. "Perla. She needs someone with height."

Dez entered the apartment to find Sherri in the same bright orange hoodie he'd seen her in at the start of the week. And in the same spot, too, sitting on the sofa, her focus on the television. She glanced over at him and smiled. "Mama's been waiting for you."

"Why do I get the feeling I'm being set up?"

Horatio nudged him in the direction of the bedrooms. Dez took a deep breath before entering Sherri's. He'd had a glimpse of her bedroom earlier in the week, but then it had been lit by moonbeams streaming in through the window. Now it was ablaze in overhead light. Glimpses into Sherri's life could be seen, and he felt slightly abashed by them. It felt intimate in a way he'd never been with her.

He started to walk out when Perla stuck her head out of the closet. "Good, you're here." She pointed to the top shelf where she'd been standing. "Since she can't reach high right now, I'm trying to make things easier for Sherri to live on her own."

Several translucent plastic containers lined the topmost shelf. Dez plucked them off and placed them on the half-made bed. Perla nodded, then peered more closely into the closet. "Thank you."

"How's she doing?"

Perla gave a shrug. "She's convinced she can live alone again, but she still has issues with using her arms. She can't shower on her own yet. And she can't cook."

"She couldn't before the surgery."

Perla chuckled and nodded. "You got me on that one." She began to reorganize items in the closet. "I ask her how is she going to eat? Wash? She tells me I worry too much. But she isn't doing the physical therapy like she's supposed to be. She seemed so positive and gung-ho about getting back her independence, but it's like she's reverted back to being a dependent child. And don't get me started on that orange hoodie."

"She was wearing it when I was here on Monday."

"And every day since. I had to force it off her once to wash it."

Wearing the same clothing wasn't a result of the surgery, Dez knew, but he had a feeling something deeper was going on than that. He glanced around the room, noting the new baskets and plastic tubs. "So you're making her life easier, but who is helping you?" When Perla glared at him, he held up his hands. "All I'm offering is to hang out here with Sherri for the evening, so you and your husband can spend time together."

"*Sí*, that would be nice." She glanced at the containers scattered over the bed and floor. "But it will take me hours to put this away."

"Leave it to Sherri and me."

"But—"

"Trust me."

He gave her a stern look that he hoped wouldn't brook any more excuses from

Perla, and it must have worked because she gave a quick nod. "All right."

He put his arm around her shoulder and steered her from the bedroom to the living room, where Sherri and her dad were watching golf. He overlooked this other change in his friend and pulled out his wallet. He put a few twenties in Perla's hand. "For dinner."

Sherri frowned at him. "What are you doing?"

"Giving your mom and dad the night off." When Perla tried to give the money back, he shook his head. "Nope, dinner is on me tonight. Consider it repayment for all the meals you cooked for me."

Horatio rose from the sofa and placed a kiss on the top of Sherri's head. "We'll be back by ten, *mija*."

Dez argued. "Midnight. You two go out and have some fun. I insist."

Perla bit her lip and looked at Sherri, who seemed to have deflated. She turned her gaze back to Dez. "Maybe tonight isn't a good night."

"It's perfect. If Sherri thinks that she can be on her own, then she needs to let you go out for a while." He put his arm around her again and urged her toward the front door. "We'll be just fine. You don't have to worry."

Horatio jingled his car keys as he waited for Perla to grab her purse and kiss Sherri. Finally, they were gone. Sherri scowled at him. "What was all that about?"

Dez checked the peephole to make sure Perla and Horatio had left. He faced Sherri and crossed his arms over his chest. "I don't want them to hear the chewing out I'm going to give you."

Sherri frowned. "Chew me out?"

"You deserve one." A big one if he could manage it.

"I'm recovering from surgery."

"You're sliding into a dark place, Sherri, and I for one won't let it happen." He crossed the space that separated them and took a seat next to her on the sofa. "I get it. All of this is bad, but get off your butt and do something about it."

"You don't know what you're talking about."

Did she think he was blind? He could see the toll this disease was taking on her. Her body may be healing, but her mind needed an infusion of hope and faith. And he'd be the man to do it. That is, he would if she would let him. "When's the last time you did your PT exercises?"

"Mama tattled." Sherri's scowl deepened. "I can't. It hurts."

"So did getting shot, but you bounced back from that faster than anyone expected."

"Because I was dealing with finding out I have cancer."

"Had cancer." Did she not see that she was more than her body? That she could conquer the invader that had entered her life and threatened it? "And that's not an excuse."

She turned her back to him and focused on the television. "But it's true."

He reached over and snatched the remote from the coffee table. No more television. "Are you going to be that person, really? The one who gives up before even trying?"

Sherri squirmed away from him and looked him square in the eye. "I am trying! But you don't know what it's like to wake up feeling like there's two rocks sitting on your chest. To not be able to use your arms. To have to depend on everyone else."

"We have to fight with you to take a shower. To change your clothes."

At this, she pulled the sleeves of the hoodie past her fingers. "I like this hoodie. It brings me comfort."

"Okay, but maybe switch it up with some of the other clothes hanging in your closet." He stood and held out his hand. "In fact, let's go look at them." She burrowed farther into the sofa. He sighed and closed his eyes. "I promised your mother we'd put away all the stuff she took out of your closet. Don't make me a liar."

Sherri hesitated, but struggled to stand without his help. Finally on her feet, she pushed past him and down the hallway. He followed behind her. "And that's another thing. Your mom is trying to make your life easier, and you're sitting back doing nothing?"

"I help."

"How are you helping by sitting on the sofa watching golf?"

She didn't answer this, but entered her bedroom. "She didn't have to do all this. I only made the comment that I wasn't going to be able to reach the things on the top shelf."

Dez put his hands on his hips and stared at her. "She's working so hard to put you back together, so why are you resisting? Why the pity party?"

Sherri paused, her gaze on the floor littered with belts and scarves. She slowly crouched and picked up a black shoe. Her voice, when it came, sounded small. "Is that what I'm doing?"

"What do you think?"

She let a tear slip down her cheek, but didn't reach up to wipe it away. She didn't even look at him, but focused on the closet. She slowly sat on the edge of her bed. "You're right."

He hated being the tough guy on her, but being soft hadn't worked so far. She needed to be shaken up. A warrior could pause and reflect, but she didn't give up so easily. Didn't let the circumstances stop her journey. He stood in front of her, held out his hand. "So do something about it."

Sherri put her hand in his, then rose to her feet and kicked at one of the empty plastic tubs. "Would you help me with this?"

"In a heartbeat."

Together they sorted things into containers and then placed the containers where it made sense to Sherri. Once they'd tidied the bedroom, they returned to the living room, where he assisted her with her PT exercises. He held his hands out in front of him so she could raise her arms and touch her fingers to his. She walked her fingers up the wall by the front door until she could get her reach to a new height, farther than when she'd started. She even took a shower and changed into a yellow button-down top and clean leggings before their pizza arrived.

Settled on the sofa with slices of pizza, they watched an action movie on television. Horatio and Perla returned shortly before midnight with smiles on their faces and in their eyes. "Have a good time?" Sherri asked them.

Perla stared at her. "You changed your clothes."

She gave them both a smile. "And showered on my own."

"Oh, *mija*. How do you feel?" her mom asked.

Sherri looked at Dez then to her mom. "Better. Thanks to Dez."

"I just nudged you," he said.

"More like shoved." She got up and crossed the room to stand in front of her parents. "I'm going to stop feeling sorry for myself and actually do something about this. I promise."

Horatio wrapped his arms around her and pulled Perla into the embrace. "My girl is coming back," he said.

CHAPTER SIX

SHERRI GRABBED THE bright orange hoodie from her closet, then put it back on the rack and chose a lime-green top that zipped up the front and a pair of her favorite jeans. She dressed quickly and walked down the hallway to find her mom scrambling eggs and singing along to the radio. She wished she could do the same, but the doubts that crowded her mind kept her from joining in. She took a seat at the counter and sipped from a glass of orange juice that was already waiting for her.

Mama turned and smiled at her. “Ready for the doctor?”

Sherri nodded and put her juice glass back on the counter. “I can’t shake this bad feeling about what he’s going to tell us today.”

“Let’s not worry before we get there.”

“I’m letting you know now that I’m

going to fight this with everything I've got. I don't care what he says because I'm going to push for aggressive treatment."

Mama paused in stirring the eggs and looked sharply at Sherri. "You're thinking of your tia Connie."

Her aunt by marriage had died from breast cancer almost twenty years before. There hadn't been a day that had passed since the surgeon had told Sherri about the diagnosis that she hadn't thought about Tia Connie. "She fought and she still died."

"You were thirteen at the time. What do you know about what she did?" Mama switched her attention back to the skillet of eggs. "Have you spoken to Mateo?"

"You know he doesn't talk about his mom."

Mama served the eggs and placed Sherri's plate in front of her before adding salt and pepper to her own breakfast. She finally looked up at Sherri. "Times were different then. So much has changed since Connie was treated. There's a better chance of survival."

"Especially if I push for the most I can get. Chemo. Radiation. Whatever it is."

"Why don't you wait until you hear what the doctor has to say before you say such things?"

"Fine." Sherri picked up her fork and scooped up some eggs. Her body had betrayed her by allowing the cancer in without telling her. She'd use every weapon she could find because she wouldn't be fooled again.

She took a bite of eggs despite the nauseated feeling in her tummy, then put her fork down. "It's time, Mama."

Her mom glanced at her watch. "We have at least another hour before we have to leave."

"I meant, it's time for you to go back home."

Mama shook her head. "Oh, I don't think you're ready to be alone yet."

"Yes, I am." Sherri reached out and touched her mom's hand. "You have been so good to me. So strong for me. But I need to stand on my own, and I'm ready."

Mama squeezed her hand. "What if I'm not ready?" She swallowed, and Sherri could see tears glistening in her eyes. "I don't want to leave you."

"You'll only be two miles away."

"You know what I mean. What if something happens, and I can't get to you in time?" Mama touched her cheek. "I can't do much to fight cancer for you, but I can be here to cook and clean for you."

She was making this harder on Sherri, but she needed to stand her ground. She needed to become more independent and take care of herself. Now. "I'll still need you, Mama, but I have to do this. Please."

Mama dropped her hand. She peered into her eyes, and Sherri steeled herself from giving in to her fears and asking her mother to stay. Finally, Mama agreed. "Okay, *mija*. I'll call your *padre* to come and pick me up after the doctor's appointment."

"Thank you."

THE NURSE TOOK her vitals before handing her the familiar light blue paper vest. "Strip from the waist up. Opening in the front."

Sherri changed, then took a seat on the examination table. Mama held the notebook and tapped the pen on the page while they waited for the surgeon. She gave a sigh and started drawing circles. "Lulu's wedding invitation arrived yesterday, your dad says. It's next month. Are you going?"

Sherri considered it. Another cousin's wedding where she'd show up without a date. Her well-meaning aunts would offer to set her up with every eligible bachelor they knew—their neighbors, coworkers' sons, acquaintances. And for an added bonus, she'd now have to face the looks of pity because of the cancer. "I don't know how I'll be feeling."

"You should go. Take Dez."

He had accompanied her before to these family weddings, but just like she needed to send Mama home so she could stand on her own two feet, she needed to keep her distance from him. To set some boundaries before things got fuzzier and more confusing than they already were. "Maybe. We'll see."

The exam room door opened, and Dr. VanGilder entered. He shook first Mama's hand and then hers. "Let's take a look at your incisions. Have the Steri-Strips fallen off?"

Sherri opened the paper vest, amazed

that she had become so used to showing her body freely. She looked down at her new chest. "For the most part."

The doctor removed the few strips that remained and nodded. "Believe it or not, you're looking good. It's been two weeks since surgery?"

Sherri said it was and glanced at Mama. "You said you'd have the biopsy results today."

Dr. VanGilder quit checking Sherri's drains and looked into her face. "I did say that." He grabbed her file and opened it. "We found more tumors than showed in your MRI and mammogram. Deep in the tissue. We also tested your lymph nodes and found cancer there, as well. I had to remove twelve of them."

Sherri took a deep breath and nodded. She'd expected news like this. "So it had spread."

"Yes, more than I'd anticipated." He handed her an appointment card. "I was able to get you in to see one of the best oncologists in this hospital, but you are free to go to one of your own choosing."

Sherri didn't know any oncologists.

Maybe she should have checked with April and Page for recommendations before coming here. She looked down at the card. "Dr. Frazier. This afternoon?"

"Because the cancer spread, we want to be aggressive. Chemo first. Radiation after." He handed her another appointment card. "This is a colleague and good friend when you're ready for the radiation. I'd recommend seeing her before chemo to get an idea of your options."

So many doctors. Was this what her life had become? One consultation after another? She put the cards in her pocket. "And I still see you?"

"I'll keep an eye on your incisions for now. Once your treatment ends, we'll start injecting your implants until they are the size you want. So you're not done with me yet." He gave her a wink.

Great.

DEZ SHOVED HIS notebook into his desk drawer and slammed it shut. He muttered a nasty word and ran a hand over his clean-shaven head. Trying to find the mole was driving him crazy. He needed more leads than what he had, but he didn't have a clue what they should be. The answer was right in front of him, but he couldn't figure it out.

He needed Sherri.

She would have read over his notes and pointed out an avenue for them to pursue. She would have seen answers, rather than more questions.

He stood and flexed his shoulders. All this sitting behind a desk was putting a strain on his neck and back. Ras glanced up at him from Sherri's desk. "Want a break?"

"I want answers." He picked up his suit coat and shrugged it on, then pulled his gun from the drawer and holstered it at his side. "I'm making another run at that DEA agent, Reilly. I'm betting he knows more than he's saying. You coming with me?"

"And leave this party? Absolutely." He grabbed his coat and gun, following Dez to the parking structure.

Dez reached his car and pressed the button to unlock the doors. Ras got in on the passenger side. "Wouldn't it be easier to call Reilly on the phone?"

Dez shook his head. "I need to see his eyes when I ask my questions."

He started the car and drove to the DEA office. Luckily, he found a vacant parking spot curbside. He then jumped out and strode to the front door. He flashed his badge at the security guard and headed toward the elevator. Ras had to run to keep up with him, but he made it to the elevator before it arrived. "How do you know he's here?" Ras asked.

"Because he's just like me. He's always working." The elevator opened and he and Ras got in. On the floor where the agency was housed, they strode down the hallway to the double glass doors. Dez entered the outer office and nodded at the receptionist. "Agent Reilly in?"

"He told me he doesn't wish to be disturbed," she answered without looking up from her computer monitor.

"He'll see us." Dez and Ras flashed their badges. "He owes me an explanation," Dez said.

She glanced up at them, then turned back to her screen without a flicker of interest. "I told you. He's busy."

"Why don't you buzz him and tell him

we're here?" Ras pointed to the phone on her desk.

She rolled her eyes, but picked up the receiver and pressed a few buttons. "Some suits are here to see you."

Dez added, "Tell him it's Desmond Jackson and Miles Rasczynski from Border Patrol."

She turned away from him and Ras and whispered into the phone, "I told him that, sir, but he insisted." She made a few noncommittal noises before hanging up the phone. She looked at them and smiled. "He's busy. He'll call you later at a more convenient time."

"Convenient for whom? I've left messages. Sent emails. And I need to speak with Agent Reilly." Dez perched on the edge of her desk. "I'll just wait here until he's free."

"You'll be waiting a long time," she replied.

Ras shrugged. "We could come back after lunch."

"Not hungry." Dez took his cell phone out and started scrolling through new emails. "I've got all day to wait."

After about fifteen minutes, an office door opened, and Reilly popped his head out to glare at Dez. "You've got five minutes."

Dez grinned at Ras and approached the office. "I thought you might try to fit me in."

Ras took a seat in front of the desk, but Dez stood, Reilly watching him. "I've already told you everything I know," Reilly said.

That he didn't believe. Any questions he had regarding the raid had been stonewalled. There was no way the DEA had shared everything. If they had, then he and Ras would be a lot further ahead than they were. Maybe the case could have been closed by now. "Convince me."

"There's nothing else to discuss."

Dez narrowed his eyes at Reilly. "And yet, we still don't know who betrayed us. It wasn't just my agents that got shot at. You had agents die. Don't you want to see justice for their sakes, at least?"

Reilly sighed and took a seat behind his desk. "I've explored all the leads we had at the time."

"Nothing's come up since? Why do I doubt you're sharing everything?"

"What about on your end? I know you're investigating this as thoroughly as I am." Reilly pointed at Ras. "New partner?"

"Who has fresh eyes that could help us crack this case open, but only if we each share everything we've got." Dez pulled a chair closer to Reilly's desk and sat. "Come on. We both know you're holding something back."

Reilly waited a full minute before he pulled out a manila folder, though he kept it on his side of the desk. "There are certain pieces of intel that are confidential and proprietary to my agency."

"So you'd rather play around like kids in a schoolyard than get answers?"

"This is strictly on a need-to-know basis."

Dez had been there, so had the other agents, so the way he figured it he had just as much need to know as Reilly. "Well, I need to know who tried to get us all killed."

Dez stared at the man, not looking away even as the agent squirmed. Finally, he pushed the folder across the desk. Dez snatched it up, perusing the information, searching for anything that might help him.

Reilly cleared his throat. "That file stays in this room. No copies. No notes. You read it, then leave."

Dez looked up. "Okay. But after I read it, Ras reads it. Only then do we leave."

"You have ten minutes." Reilly stood and walked to the window. "All my agents were cleared as you can tell on page three."

Dez focused on the information regarding each agent. "Then you think it really was Border Patrol that had the leak?"

Reilly turned and glared at him. "You said it. Not me."

"No. The only agents on my side who knew about our mission ahead of time were Sherri and myself." Dez paused. "And my captain, of course."

"Yes. Captain White, who has cousins in Canada. Cousins who have a farm that grows *more* than vegetables." Reilly leaned over Dez's shoulder. "You might want to check page seven."

Dez flipped to the spot and shook his head. "No." He read over the short report that laid out the Canadian connection in Captain White's family. "Cap would never..."

"It's all conjecture, of course."

Dez passed the file to Ras.

Captain White was like a father to his team. He wouldn't have sent them knowingly into harm's way. There had to be another source. Had to be. Dez watched as Ras read through the file, then turned back to the beginning and read it again.

Reilly gave a wan smile. "Time's up."

Ras handed the file to the agent, and stood. He looked at Dez, who gave a short nod. "If I have more questions..." Dez directed at Reilly.

"I'd take a look at your own office before you burst back into mine." Reilly opened a desk drawer and shoved the file inside. Then he went and opened the door for Dez and his partner. "Good day, gentlemen."

Dez and Ras didn't say a word as they headed back to the car. Once inside, Dez started the engine, but let it idle. He'd missed something. He was sure of that because the idea that Cap would betray them was unacceptable. Eventually, he put the car in Drive and pulled away from the curb.

Ras had taken out a notebook and started scribbling notes. When Dez switched on the radio, he reached over and turned it off. "I need silence for a minute."

Dez drummed his fingers on the steering wheel, trying to remain patient while he reviewed the facts, hoping they'd lead to a logical conclusion. But nothing made sense.

Ras put his notebook away, then switched on the radio. "He played you."

Dez kept his eyes on the road. "What? How? I don't get played."

"He distracted you with the information about Captain White so that you wouldn't find something else that was there. The truth." Ras gave a slight shrug. "I'm almost positive he didn't want us to pay attention to the contents of that file."

Possible. "You read the entire file, though. Twice. What did we miss?"

Ras flipped through his notebook. "Nowhere in any of the reports did it say for certain which way the leaked information went. It implied the person in question was providing info to the agency, but it could have been going the other way."

"So you're agreeing with Reilly?" Dez rubbed his right eye, which had started to twitch. "We're back to square one, then. Who ratted us out? And why?"

"Well, your good friend Reilly clearly wanted to implicate the captain, didn't he? That's suspicious. Maybe we should start there." Ras held up the notebook. "I tried to recreate as much of the file as I could, but I don't have a photographic memory."

"Sherri does." He hit his fist on the steering wheel. He missed her because he knew he could bust this case wide open with her on lead. He nodded toward Ras's notebook. "Could you make me a copy of your notes? I'd like her to look them over."

"Sure."

DR. FRAZIER WAS only a few years older than herself and looked as if she might have gone to school with Sherri. She had dark hair braided into cornrows that ended in green beads, pulled back into a ponytail. Sherri shook Dr. Frazier's hand and then took a seat on the examination table. "Dr. VanGilder had a lot of good things to say about you."

"Let me guess. He called me the best."

Sherri peered at her closely. "Are you?"

"Depends on who you talk to. I'd like to think so." Dr. Frazier opened her file and flipped through a few pages. She put it aside and approached her, a frown on her face. "VanGilder went over the biopsy results, then?"

Unfortunately, he had exhausted her with the details of how bad her situation appeared. But then, she hadn't chosen him as her surgeon so that she would hear the truth sugarcoated. He'd been up-front from the beginning, and she admired that. "I heard what he thought, but I want to know what you think."

"My biggest concern is that while it seems that the surgery removed all the cancer, its aggressive nature could have left surprises elsewhere. I can recommend a strong cocktail of chemotherapy drugs that should knock them out."

"Without knocking me out in the process?"

Dr. Frazier gave a soft chuckle. "That is my plan." She got out her cell phone and scrolled through a few screens before stopping on a calendar. Sherri could see it from where she was on the examination table. "We can do blood work tomorrow and start treatment in a week. Are you game?"

So soon. Just as with everything else, the doctors, nurses, technicians moved forward quickly, hoping to get an edge on the cancer. She nodded, but she didn't feel as if she was truly connected to what was happening to herself. "I will do whatever we have to do, Doctor."

"Now, that's what I like to hear." She made notes in her file, then took a blue prescription pad and wrote down several items before ripping the page off the pad and handing it to her. "Call the number on top to set up your first appointment. It will be more like a dry run. They'll go through what you should expect as well as check your blood work to make sure that everything is ready. They'll also arrange all the dates of your chemo treatment for the next three to four months. Then you'll return the following day for the actual treatment. Your initial infusion. Any questions?"

Millions. Sherri reached up and touched her head. "My hair?"

"Most people lose their hair, yes. Usually within the first few weeks of treatment." She pulled a sheet of paper out of her file. "There's a lot of possible side effects with chemotherapy. Some people have a few of them. Some have all. It depends on how your body reacts to the chemicals. We'll handle each side effect as it pops up, so don't worry. I'll get you through this."

Sherri took the sheet and read over the list of side effects. Mouth sores. Nausea and vomiting. Weight loss. Weight gain. Hot flashes. Short-term memory loss. She stopped reading and gave a big sigh. "This is…" She searched for the word, but couldn't think of what she wanted.

"Overwhelming." Dr. Frazier paused and looked down at her hands. "I get it. I'm a cancer survivor myself, and I know all the emotions and thoughts that are swirling around you right now."

"I don't even know what to worry about first."

Dr. Frazier looked up at her. "I tell you what. I'll worry about your treatment. You focus on staying positive." She held out her hand to her. "Deal?"

She shook the woman's hand, unsure how she would hold up her part of the bargain.

DEZ MADE PHOTOCOPIES of his notes as well as those he'd gotten from Ras. He folded the papers and placed them in his pocket before leaving the office for the night. It was only seven, early enough to stop by Sherri's to see how her doctor's appointment had gone.

Plus, he could ask her for her thoughts on the case.

He called Smitty and set up a reservation for the two of them to spend time at the gun range. Bribery never hurt.

He knocked on her apartment door and waited. It was late May, but the temperatures had already soared into the eighties. Probably meant that the summer would be a blistering one. The door opened, and Sherri frowned at him. "Did we have plans?"

"Smitty is waiting for us. We tee off in a half hour."

She smiled and stepped back to let him inside. "You're speaking my language."

He entered and looked around the living room. "Your mom out for the evening?"

"I sent her home this afternoon. It was time."

Despite what he'd told her the last time he was with her, the thought of her being on her own made him feel a little queasy. Worry spread through his veins. "You're sure that you're ready?"

Sherri took her purse from the kitchen counter. "I have to do it eventually. I'll just grab my gun and we can go."

Dez drove them to the gun range. He followed her inside to the counter where Smitty had laid out paper targets and ear protection. Sherri paused to purchase ammunition. Smitty handed her the box of bullets, but didn't remove his hand. "You know, my wife had breast cancer."

She glanced at Dez. "You told him?"

Smitty shook his head. "He didn't have to. I've seen you every week for the last four years, and I can tell when something is different." Sherri looked down at her flatter chest, and he took her free hand in one of his. "Semper Fi, Lopez."

She gave him a teary smile. "Thanks,

Smitty." Then she turned and walked with Dez to the cubicles he'd reserved. She took her gun from her purse and loaded a full clip into the empty chamber. She gave a sigh as she tacked a target onto the line and sent it out at a distance. "You don't know how much I needed this tonight." She put the earmuffs in place.

Dez had to look away, overcome with the wish that he could put that satisfied expression on her face himself. He cleared his throat. "Smitty said we could take all the time we need. He's missed seeing you here."

"I only hope my surgery hasn't thrown off my aim." She loosened her shoulders, then aimed her gun at the target and emptied the cartridge. She loaded another clip and started the process all over again. Nothing could affect her aim, or her determination, for that matter.

Knowing she'd be okay, he entered his cubicle and let out his aggression by shooting at a few targets.

After an hour Sherri quit and leaned against one wall. "I'm spent," she called out to him.

He removed his earmuffs and glanced over at her. The shadows under her eyes were more pronounced, so he gave a quick nod and put the safety on his gun before putting that, plus the box of extra ammunition, back into his duffel bag. "C'mon, I'll take you home."

Once inside his car, Sherri turned to face him. "Why do I get the feeling that you want something? You buttered me up with the gun range, so it must be important. What is it?"

For one crazy moment he thought about pulling her in for a kiss, to show her what he really wanted. But sense returned, and he took out the folded papers from his pocket. "You know me too well."

She accepted the pages from him and flipped through them. After a few minutes she shrugged. "Reports on the drug raid again? We've been through them already."

"I'm missing something. I know it. I need your expert eyes. I met with Reilly today at the DEA." He filled her in on the conversation as well as Ras's assertion that he had been played by the agent to jump to certain conclusions to distract him from other intel. "I was hoping you'd spot a connection we're missing."

She reviewed the notes more slowly, then pointed out one phrase to Dez. "The captain isn't the only one attached to the drug raid who has Canadian connections. I think Ras was right. Reilly was trying to distract you. I wish we could get our hands on that DEA report."

"Ras tried to reconstruct as much of it as he could. Did you see the bit about how the DEA did get a tip-off that the cartel might know we were coming, but no one felt it was necessary to share that with those of us who'd be there?"

She sighed and shuffled the pages, scanning the notes. "You need to pursue that one name that pops up in a couple of places. That Omarian guy was mentioned more than once. Could mean something. It'd be a good place to start."

"But who is Omarian? I don't remember an agent by that name, do you?"

Sherri shook her head and looked up at him, her nose only inches from his. He swallowed as he peered into her eyes, feeling pieces of his heart falling away. He reached out and pushed a strand of her hair behind her ear. She licked her lips, and his gaze dropped to her mouth.

"Dez?"

He suddenly realized she'd said his name a couple times. He sat back in the driver's seat. "You said you loved me."

She frowned at him. "I did."

"So are we going to talk about it? Because it seems to me that we should."

"You know I love you. You're my best friend."

"That's not what you meant."

Sherri glanced out the window, looking away from him. "It's nothing."

"Seems like something, but you don't want to talk about it." He put the key in the ignition, but didn't start the car. "We're friends and partners, but if you want different things now, you need to tell me."

She turned back to look at him. "I want us to be like we always have." She put her hand on his shoulder. "I don't want to change things right now. I need you and I to be one of the normal things in my life. Can you understand that?"

He didn't understand what was between

them. He loved her, too. He wanted to explore those feelings with her, but maybe she was right. Their timing was off. When she was cured and healthy again, they could figure this out. Until then, he'd do what she wanted.

When he nodded, she yawned widely and covered her mouth with her hand.

"You must be tired. I should get you home."

She settled back into the passenger seat. "Are you okay?"

He started the car and put it into Drive. "Yeah. Just tired, I guess."

"We can talk about the case later. Can I keep these?" She held up the notes he'd given her.

"Those are your copies."

She tucked the papers into her purse. Dez rubbed his head. What had he been thinking? Well, he knew what he'd been thinking. He thought if he could have just one kiss, then this could get out of his system.

Silence descended on them until it became uncomfortable. He searched for a safe topic of conversation. "How did your doctor's appointment go today?"

"Which one?" Her shoulders drooped and she stared at the floor. "I start chemo next week."

"So soon?"

"The sooner I start, the sooner it's over." She ran a hand through her hair. "This is going to sound crazy, but the thing I'm most worried about is losing my hair."

He glanced at her. "It will grow back."

"That's not the point. I can lose my breasts, and only those close to me will know the difference. But losing my hair? Everyone will know I'm sick."

"Those who love you already know."

"And that's the other thing. Another cousin's getting married. Lulu."

He vaguely recognized the name. "Mateo's sister?"

She nodded and shifted in her seat as if uncomfortable. "I'll be a month into chemo. I don't want my family to give me those looks." She stared and pointed at him. "Exactly like that. Pity."

"I don't pity you."

She rolled her eyes, so he screwed his

features up and made a goofy face. “They could look at you like this.”

She laughed and swatted his leg. “You know what I mean.”

He braked for the red light then put an arm around her shoulders. “Tell you what. If it makes you feel better, we can shave our heads together. They won’t be able to tell us apart.”

“Not much of a sacrifice for you when you’re already bald.” She giggled, but then her smile faltered, and she covered her face with her hands. “I’m being silly, I know. But I keep asking myself what else am I going to lose after this is all over?”

He pulled her closer to his side. “You won’t lose me. I guarantee that.”

LEATHER HIT LEATHER as the softball team warmed up for practice. One line of players threw the ball across to others, then back as Dez scanned his clipboard, deciding who would be playing what position. It was the first practice for the summer league of Border Patrol agents. He’d hoped that Sherri would at least show up to prove to the rest of the team that she was going to be okay.

Instead, her absence seemed to be felt by each player. They glanced at every car that pulled into the parking lot, but none were hers. His eyes drifted to the rows of cars beyond the ball field.

"All right, everyone. Bring it in!" He clapped his hands as they neared. He looked around the huddle. "You all know Sherri is going to be out this season, so I'm looking for a cocaptain to assist me."

A hand shot up. Perkins. That surprised him since he didn't really know the guy that well. "How is she doing?"

Oh. "She's recovering from surgery and will be going through chemo soon. So please keep her in your prayers and thoughts."

Another hand. "Does she need anything?"

Good question. How do you help someone who didn't want it? "You'd have to ask her." He looked around the group. "Now, who is willing to help me manage this team for the next three months?"

"I could give a hand."

Everyone turned and shouted as Sherri joined them. She gave some hugs to people who approached her. She pulled her baseball hat around so that the bill stuck out in back. "I checked with the head of the league, and I don't have to play in the field in order to cocaptain as long as we have enough team members without me."

As much as he wanted her to be here, what would it be like once she started chemo? What if being around all these people made her sicker? There were possible complications from the treatment. The chemo attacking the cancer cells would also decimate her immune system. She'd be susceptible to the simplest germ. Dez shook his head. "Maybe that's not the best idea."

"Dez, I checked it out. I'll be able to sit on the bench and still help you." She put her hands on her hips. "We have plenty of players on the roster."

"Let's run bases and then we'll have batting practice." He pointed to Sherri as everyone glanced at each other, then left the two of them. "I really wanted you to be here tonight since you're feeling well, but what if you take a turn for the worse? I'm going to have to put my foot down. Sorry, but I'm not convinced this is for the best."

"Of course it is. I need this."

"No, what you need is to take care of yourself."

She touched his arm, and he tried to ignore the tingle it brought. "Me sitting on the bench isn't going to hurt."

"Once you start chemo, your immune system will be compromised, and you're going to surround yourself with a bunch of germy people?" He shook his head again. That wasn't going to happen. Not on his watch.

"I also checked with my doctor, who agreed that me being involved with an activity like this would help me rather than do me harm. Dez, you're overreacting again."

He put a hand on her shoulder, and she backed away from him so that his arm fell to his side. "I can't let you do this."

Her eyes flashed with anger. "Let me? Last I checked I still have a choice about what I do with my life. You don't get a say."

"Why do you have to be so stubborn?"

The words came out louder than he'd intended, and some of the runners paused to look at them. He closed his eyes and scrubbed a hand over his jaw. "Sherri, please be reasonable. I'm trying to protect you."

"I don't need protection."

"Obviously you do. You're about to throw away your health for a few lousy ball games?"

"This is about more than a game." She grabbed his wrist with one hand. "I told you before that I need to have some kind of normal. Please. If it gets to be too much, then we can find a replacement." She put her other hand on his chest. "Dez, please."

He couldn't resist the look in her eyes, the pleading that poured out of them. Having her in his sights, he realized that he couldn't deny her this small thing. "Fine. But if at any point, it becomes too much for you to handle or you're too sick, then you're out."

She gave a smile. "Agreed."

He let out a sigh and thrust the clipboard at her. "I made a list about who's playing which position, but I'm sure you'll have your own ideas."

She looked down and grimaced at his

handwriting. "You bet I do. You run the practice, and I'll fix this mess."

"It isn't that bad."

She raised one eyebrow at this, then walked to the bench. Dez took the field and called everyone to home base. "Okay, Sherri will be cocaptain as much as she can. Please be careful around her. She's still fragile."

"No, I'm not!" she shouted from the sidelines.

He ignored her and lowered his voice so that only his teammates could hear him. "She's also very determined to do this. Okay, Perkins, you'll lead us off. Grab a bat and you'll be followed by Sara. Sherri's got everyone's positions, so check with her and let's have a good practice."

SHERRI YAWNED AND leaned against the wall of the dugout. She closed her eyes for a moment. She felt a hand on her forehead and opened her eyes to find Dez scrutinizing her. "You're warm."

"It's a hot June day and we've been out here for over two hours. Of course I'm warm."

Dez stood and started toward the field. "I'm calling practice and you're going home."

She jumped up, shaking her head. She approached him and put a hand on his arm to hold him back. "I closed my eyes for one minute. I'm okay."

He called the team in and sent everyone home with reminders about the next practice and the date of their first game. Sherri started to gather the equipment that littered the dugout. She waved at several people who called out goodbyes, then waited for Dez, who retrieved the bases and added them to the bag he was carrying.

He hefted the heavy bag over his shoulder and motioned with his head to the parking lot. Sherri fell into step behind him, carrying the clipboard and a small bag of softballs. She'd needed to prove that she was still the same strong warrior he'd always known. Cancer wasn't going to change her. But would he listen?

When they reached their cars, Dez unloaded the equipment bag into the back of his truck and took the bag of balls from her. He unlocked the door and stood there, the sun setting behind him, lining his features in golden shadows. She opened her mouth to tell him what she'd been thinking, but she changed her mind when her gaze met his.

He coughed and cleared his throat. "I guess I'll see you before your first chemo appointment in a few days."

She left him and started to walk toward her car. Hearing him call her name, she stopped and he narrowed the gap between them. "I don't know if this is the best idea for you, but if your doctor gave his approval, then I'm on board. I guess. But I mean it. If it gets to be too much, then you're out. Got it?"

"I needed this tonight, Dez. I needed to be around people who are living their lives like they always do. Because I don't have that right now." She glanced away, upset that her eyes burned with tears that she refused to show or let fall.

She had to be strong. If only to prove to herself and not just Dez that she was still tough. "I don't like anything about my life right now and it felt good to escape that for a couple of hours."

"You can't escape your own life, Ace. You need to face it and fight."

Isn't that what she was doing by trying to hang on to some normalcy? To tell the cancer that it might take her breasts, but it wouldn't change her? That she was still Sherri, cocaptain of the softball team and strong warrior? But she took a breath and smiled at his admonition. "You always have to have the last word. Even when we're talking about *my* life."

He put both hands on her shoulders. "I'm overprotective. I get that. But it's because I care so much. I don't know what I'd do if I lost you."

She gazed into his eyes and swallowed. The pain staring back at her looked much like how she felt. She didn't know how she could survive losing him, either. "I'll be careful. I promise."

"I'm holding you to that." He pulled her in for a hug and rested his head on top of hers. "Take care of yourself, Ace."

"You got it, Captain."

He kissed the top of her head, turned and strode to his truck.

CHAPTER SEVEN

SHERRI DRESSED AS if she was really going to work: cream-colored silk sleeveless blouse and navy skirt with heels. She decided to forgo makeup and let her hair hang down her back.

She made coffee and filled the travel mug—part of her usual morning routine—and headed out the door, purse over her shoulder, gun holstered to her side.

When she arrived at the office, the captain didn't seem surprised to see her. Actually, her appearance seemed to put a touch of wariness in his expression as if he'd been expecting this fight. She strode into his office and shut the door behind her. "We need to talk."

He looked her over and shook his head. "No."

"You don't even know what I'm going to ask."

Cap stared at her, one eyebrow raised. “You’re not coming back on duty unless you’re sitting at a desk. You’ve only been out three weeks, and you still have three more to go.”

Sherri pouted and slumped into the chair before his massive oak desk. She watched him as he examined something on his computer screen. She gathered her courage, leaned forward and tapped one finger on the desk. “You need me out there.”

“No,” Cap said, never taking his eyes off the screen. “I need you healthy and alive. And you’ll do what I tell you to do. And do you know why? Because I’m the boss. Not you.”

“You know, I’ve always assumed I’d have your job one day.” She figured that another five years of exemplary service, and she would be in line for a promotion. But if cancer took her out for a few months, would that affect her career in the long-term? Would she lose another piece of herself to this disease?

“There’s no reason you still can’t,” he said. The captain stood and came around the desk and sat on the edge. “This is just a temporary setback, Lopez. I have you on the schedule starting in a few weeks once your surgeon approves it, and not a day before. You'll be on desk duty until further notice."

She made a face at this. "I'm better than desk duty."

"That may be, but you're not cleared to be out in the field right now." He returned to sit behind his desk. "Dez says that he's been feeding you his notes, trying to get your perspective."

She hoped she hadn't gotten Dez in trouble by asking him to keep her in the loop. "Is that an issue?"

"Why would it be? We need to find out who betrayed us and almost got you killed before it happens again. You're my best agent, and I do need you on that case. Even if it's from behind a desk."

She gave him a weak smile and tapped her foot rapidly on the carpet. "It's not fair."

"Life's not fair, Lopez." The captain went back to looking at his computer screen. He asked, "Now, is there more to this social call, or can I get on with my work?"

Sherri rose and crossed her arms over

her chest, ignoring the twinge of pain caused by her scars. "I will be back."

He looked up at her. "I'm counting on it."

She left his office and stopped at Dez's desk, but it was empty, as was hers. He must be out on a call with his partner. She grabbed a Post-it note and wrote a quick couple of words, then placed it in the center of his computer screen. At her desk, she ran a hand along the cold, empty surface. Promising she'd be back soon, she hurried from the station and drove toward the hospital to meet April and Page for lunch.

The Chinese restaurant next to the hospital was packed, but Sherri was able to snag a table before her friends showed. Page walked in first, and Sherri stood and waved her over. The ob/gyn nurse in pastel pink scrubs huffed as she took a seat and slipped off her pink zebra print surgical cap to reveal her bald head. "Someday, this job will kill me."

April arrived and put her hand on Page's shoulder. "You have hormonal mothers. I have knife-wielding patients off their bipolar meds."

Page looked up at April. "Are we really going to compare jobs?"

April screwed up her face in thought, then broke into a smile. "No, because I'd win hands down. Every time."

Page groaned and opened the menu, muttering under her breath about the egos of some doctors. Sherri opened her own menu to hide her smile at the way these friends teased each other. She knew what she was going to order, so she put her menu down and sipped her ice water.

April seemed to be studying her. "You're looking really good."

"That's because I haven't started chemo yet," Sherri replied and fiddled with her silverware. She didn't know why it was so hard to talk about this, but suddenly the topic of her cancer seemed taboo. Almost as if it embarrassed her.

April reached over and touched her hand. "Come on, it's okay, whatever it is you're feeling."

Sherri gave a half-hearted shrug. "Talking won't change anything."

April shook her head, her short curls moving in motion. "Of course it doesn't change anything, but it might make you feel better. When I first got diagnosed, I visited the Hope Center to get information, but I stayed on because of the camaraderie between the women who had been there before me. They helped me by opening up about their own experiences and allowing me to share about mine. I left feeling a little more confident, less scared about what lies ahead."

All Sherri felt was fear. Confidence had disappeared with her diagnosis; she searched daily to find the strength to move on. "And what does lie ahead?"

"A lot of vomit." Page looked up from her menu with an expression that gave her words gravity. "No hair. Runny nose. Weird rashes, although that will probably come later with the radiation."

April swatted at her friend. "So much for making her less scared, Page."

"She needs to know the truth." Page turned back to Sherri. "But the truth is, it won't be like you're imagining. You've got all these worst-case scenarios in your head right now. But I'm telling you that reality will be much different."

"Better?" Sherri certainly hoped so, since what she imagined was pretty awful.

Page shrugged. "Not better. Just different. This is my second time through this cancer, and I can honestly say that each time was unique. You don't know what to expect, so don't. Go with whatever happens."

That didn't sound very reassuring, unfortunately. The waiter arrived to take their orders, so the conversation shifted. While Page spoke to the server, April reached across the table and touched Sherri's hand again. The small kindness wasn't lost on Sherri. "Page hasn't had it easy, so she's a little harsh."

"Little?" Page made a noise with her mouth that expressed her disgust. "I don't do anything halfway."

April smiled. "Okay, a lot harsh. But she knows what she's talking about." When the waiter left, she brought out a bright pink gift bag from beneath the table and handed it to Sherri. "This is from the two of us. Like a goody bag to help you with chemo."

Sherri peered inside the bag and gasped.

She pulled out a soft yellow blanket and rubbed her cheek against it. "I love it."

"In case the chemo room is cold."

Page gave a snort. "And it will be. Guaranteed. No matter how many times you ask them to raise the temperature."

Sherri also found socks, lip balm, peppermint hard candies, lotion and a selection of magazines and crossword puzzles in the goody bag. "This is great. Thank you both."

April gave a satisfied smile. "There are more things we can recommend, but these items are the fun ones to pick out."

From the bottom of the bag, Sherri pulled out a cloth journal with a pink ribbon drawn on the front. "To write that book I've always meant to?"

"To help you find the words about what you're going through." When Page groaned, April frowned at her. "I know you think it's all part of my mumbo jumbo, Page, but it really helped me get through my treatment." She yanked a similar journal from her purse. "It was hard to put what I was feeling onto these pages when I started out, but it began to comfort me as

I wrote things down. As if I wasn't alone and I'd have something of me to leave behind if the worst happened." She ran a hand over its cover. "I learned a lot about myself. And if cancer has a positive side, then that was mine." Sherri could see a glistening in April's eyes. "Maybe it will help you, too."

"Thank you." Sherri put all of the items back in the gift bag, knowing she'd never received such a treasure. One that was sure to keep giving in the weeks and months to come.

DEZ DRIBBLED THE basketball, then passed it to Luke. The boy pivoted and made a perfect three-point shot at the basket. He held up his hands in victory. "That's two, old man. You owe me dinner."

Dez lifted one eyebrow. "We've moved from ice cream to dinner?"

"I schooled you on this court, so I'm thinking that I deserve a burger and fries."

Luke watched him, his eyes daring him to refuse him. Dez rubbed his sweaty head with his shirt then put it back on. "Sounds like a plan."

Dez drove them to a place near his own

neighborhood where they knew him by name since he ate there so often. He signaled to the owner, Pete, for two ice waters and chose a corner booth and slid in. Luke sat across from him and glanced around the half-empty diner. "This is a nice place."

Dez forgot how much of his life he took for granted. Pete's greasy spoon was far from four-star dining, but for Luke it was as if they had white tablecloths and fancy china. Pete brought over menus, but Dez waved them away. "We're here for two of your finest cheeseburgers with the works."

Pete dutifully wrote it on an order pad. "We fixed our malted machine if you're interested in a milk shake."

Luke glanced up at Dez, who nodded. "Make mine a vanilla."

Luke shook his head. "Chocolate. Please."

Pete wrote that down, too, and walked away to put in their orders. Dez noticed Luke as he touched the silverware, the bottles of ketchup and mustard, the tiny packets of jelly stacked in a container. A kid in the candy store had nothing on Luke in a diner. Dez put an arm along the back of the seat. "How's your mom doing?"

Luke's grin faded, and he shrugged. "Okay, I guess. She cried when I told her about graduation." He fiddled with his fork. "She dropped out at ninth grade, you know?"

Dez nodded. He also knew that Luke's mom, Donna, had gone back to get her GED after she'd given birth to him. She was a survivor, much like the scrawny kid in front of him. "She's proud of you. So am I."

Another shrug. "It's no big deal."

Dez leaned down to get into the boy's line of sight. "Don't fool yourself. This is only the beginning for you, kid. So why don't we talk about what's after high school?"

Luke screwed his face up. "You talking college? Because that's not happening for me."

"Why not?" Luke had the brains for it as well as the drive to succeed.

"You need serious cash for that, and I don't have two dimes." The boy slumped in the booth. "I'll probably get a job. Help Mom out with the bills."

Luke sounded resigned to his fate, but Dez wanted something more for him. And he had a feeling that Luke did, too. "Is that what you really want?"

"Since when does what I want mean something?"

Dez couldn't help it; his anger sprang forward. "Don't talk like that! There's no limit to what you can accomplish if you put your mind to it."

"Right."

If the kid's eyes rolled any more, they'd fall out and spin around the floor. Dez decided to take another tack. "What about your friends? What are they doing after high school?"

"You mean those who are actually graduating?" He gestured as if he didn't care. "Working. Hanging out with their baby mamas."

"And you want to be like them?"

Luke leaned back in the booth and stared out the window, avoiding Dez's eyes. "I know what you're trying to do, Dez. But I don't have a lot of options like you did."

That was where he was wrong. "I wasn't much different from you at your age. Tall and skinny. I had no money. No family except for my foster dad. And no plans beyond surviving that day without getting my butt beat. Options weren't exactly lying around waiting for me to pick them up off the street."

Luke turned back, nodding. "And then you joined the marines."

He said it as if he'd heard the story many times before, but Dez needed him to hear it with a new perspective. "Yes. I joined the Corps. And suddenly, doors opened for me."

Luke raised his head and looked at him fully in the face. "And they paid for your college?"

Dez nodded and let it sink in. "What would you like to do, if there were no obstacles? If there was nothing to hold you back?"

Luke shrugged and looked out the window again. A world of worries rested in the gaze he kept on the parking lot even as Pete brought their shakes. He also put a metal tumbler in front of Luke. "I accidentally made more than what would fit in the glass."

Luke thanked Pete, then peeled the wrapper off a straw. He placed it in the shake and sucked down about an inch. He winced and put a hand to his forehead. "Brain freeze."

Dez smiled and took smaller sips of his own milk shake. His phone buzzed, and he glanced at the screen. A text from Sherri. He swiped to read the full message.

Need your help. You free?

Eating dinner with Luke.

After?

Sure. What do you need?

A new body. Ha-ha. I'll settle for yours.

Dez felt a fine line of perspiration form above his lip. She wanted his body?

Luke tried to read Dez's screen. "Your girlfriend?"

Dez was the one to shrug this time. "My

friend who is a girl, yes. She needs my help with something."

"Oh." Luke played with the straw wrapper. "That mean we gotta leave now?"

Dez texted back that he would come over after they'd eaten dinner. "And miss our burgers? Sherri understands the needs of a man's stomach."

When Pete brought their meals to the table, Dez ordered another burger and fries to go for Sherri. He might as well feed her on top of whatever help she needed.

SHERRI FROWNED AT the box on a shelf at the top of the coat closet, trying to figure out how to get it down without injuring herself or what was inside. They must have forgotten this one when they'd been rearranging her space.

A knock on the front door told her the cavalry had arrived. She opened the door and paused at the sight of two men. "You brought company."

Dez handed her a plastic container. "And dinner." He stepped inside, then turned to the young man. "Come on in, she won't bite."

Sherri held out her free hand. “You must be Luke.”

He shook it with surprising firmness. “And you’re Sherri. Sorry about the cancer.”

He’d told him? She shot Dez a look but he was scoping out the kitchen. “What did you need me to do?” he asked her.

She pointed to the box in her coat closet. “I still can’t raise my arms that high. Besides, it definitely weighs more than a gallon of milk.”

Luke scrunched up his eyebrows. “Why does it matter how much milk weighs?”

“It’s about five pounds, which is the most I’m allowed to lift right now.”

Dez grabbed the box from the shelf and carried it to the kitchen counter. He groaned. “Did you pack bricks in there?”

She gave a sigh, some from relief, more from pleasure. “Thanks. I needed something in here.”

She lifted the lid, and both Dez and Luke peered at the contents. DVDs, CDs and books filled the box. She lifted out the movie she’d been thinking about earlier and clasped it to her chest. Dez looked questioningly at her. "A cartoon?"

"It's a classic film about the imagined life of toys." She gave a shrug. "It always cheers me up."

Luke peered at her, and she had the feeling that the young man had eyes that didn't miss anything. "I remember that movie. Does it help if you're feelin' sad?"

"It does. A little. I need something simple to entertain and uplift me."

"A lot of fancy words in that sentence." The boy turned to Dez. "So we helped her. Can we go?"

Dez held up a finger to signal they should wait. "This was all you needed?" he asked her.

Sherri pointed at the container. "Movie *and* a dinner. What more could I want?" He watched her, and she tried not to squirm under such close observation. "Unless you want to join me? I could use the company."

He glanced at Luke. "I've got to get him home before his mom starts worrying, but I can come back."

She shook her head and waved his offer off as if everything was fine. When they'd worked together so intimately, she never thought about having to say goodbye to him every day. But now that she was home alone, she craved time with Dez. Not that she could tell him such things. "I'll be okay. Thanks for the food." She reached up and kissed him on the cheek, then to Luke she held out her hand. "Nice to finally meet you."

He gave her a polite smile. "You, too. Good luck with the cancer."

"Thanks." She showed them out.

LUKE SHOOK HIS head at Dez, admonishing him, as he fastened his seat belt. "I thought you said you two were just friends? How are you not hitting that?"

Dez kept his eyes on the parking lot behind him as he backed out of the space. "First of all, don't talk like that about women. And second, what are you talking about?"

"She called you over just to get a movie from a box? Please."

Dez turned and looked at the boy, but he couldn't understand the words. "I told you we're friends."

“Mmm-hmm. Listen, I’m no genius, but that girl wanted you bad. And you blew her off like she meant nothing.”

His relationship with Sherri was built on honesty. She would have insisted he stay if she’d really wanted him to. And he never would have dismissed her as if it meant nothing. “I didn’t blow her off.”

“She played it like she was okay with you leaving. But trust me she wants you to come back.”

Dez shook his head, amazed that the teen had noticed so much in so little time. “How do you know this?”

The boy gave a half shrug. “I’ve watched my mom with guys. She thinks I’m too young to notice stuff, but I’ve got eyes. I know how she plays the game.”

“Sherri isn’t playing anything.”

“Maybe I’m wrong, then.”

“We’re just friends.” He said the words, but something in his gut told him that wasn’t quite true.

He dropped Luke off at his apartment, then started the drive back to his own place. He was a mile from home when he took a hard left turn and drove back toward

Sherri's apartment. He stopped at the store and bought ice cream, then parked in the lot. When he got to her door, he raised his hand to knock, but paused. Was Luke right about Sherri wanting more from him than friendship? Could he really have what he most wanted? Only one way to find out.

She answered the door and smiled when she saw him. "You came back."

She genuinely looked as if she was happy to see him. Words got stuck in his throat, and he stared at her openmouthed before thrusting the ice cream into her hands. "Yes. I did."

Oh, that was smooth. He followed her inside and into the kitchen, where she pulled out spoons and handed one to him. "You don't have to keep buying me ice cream."

He flipped the spoon between his fingers. "I couldn't think of anything else."

He took a spoonful of ice cream when she held out the open carton to him. He pondered Luke's words again as he looked at her, wanting to ask her, afraid of her answer. She brushed past him to return to the living room sofa and the television where the movie had been paused. She patted the spot beside her. If that wasn't an invitation, he'd eat the cardboard container rather than the ice cream.

He sat next to her, and she turned the movie back on. She snuggled into the sofa and pulled a thin cotton blanket over her shoulders. He helped her adjust the blanket around her. "Are you cold?"

"Ever since the surgery, I seem to get chilly a lot. I've taken to having a blanket next to the sofa just for these moments."

Dez opened his arms and pulled her to his side. "Here. I'll warm you up."

She opened her mouth, and he hoped it wasn't to protest. But she gave in and settled beside him, resting her head on his shoulder. They ate from the ice cream container and watched the movie. They didn't require any words. Being together like this was enough.

For now.

As the film ended, Sherri sighed. "Thanks for being such a good friend. I didn't know how to tell you how much I needed you here tonight."

A good friend. Right.

Dez swallowed the disappointment. "I've

always told you I'm here for you. Even when you say you don't need me."

She looked up at him, and he noticed that she had a smear of chocolate on one side of her mouth. He reached out with his pinkie and wiped it away. Sherri's tongue came out between her lips and followed the trail his finger had made. He stared at her mouth, shook his head and cleared his throat. "Sorry. You had some ice cream just there."

"Oh."

The moment expanded as they looked at each other. He wanted to kiss her then, but she seemed scared. She hurriedly got up from the sofa and retreated to the kitchen. She came back with a paper in her hands and gave it to him. "Can I ask another favor?"

She could ask for the moon if she wanted to, and he would find a way to get it for her. "You ask a lot."

She chuckled, and he longed to kiss the smile on her face. "And this is a big ask."

"Whatever you need."

She pointed to the paper. "Be my date to my cousin's wedding next month."

"Date?" He read the invitation over, hoping that his heart would start again. Could she be asking what he thought she was? Had she finally seen him as a man and not just a friend? Or would she insist that nothing had changed between them when he couldn't deny that everything had?

She elbowed him in the chest, and he rubbed the spot though it hadn't hurt. "You know what I mean."

Unfortunately, he did know. He felt as if they were on a roller coaster where in one minute he thought she wanted more, then in the next she insisted on being just friends. He tried to keep the regret from his voice. "I'd be happy to go with you."

She reached up and touched her scalp. "Even if I'm bald by then?"

He tried to think of something to say, but there seemed to be more going on than what he could put into words. He reached out and touched her hair. "I told you. We'll be a matching set."

CHAPTER EIGHT

SHERRI PULLED THE bright orange hoodie on, then zipped it up the front. It was her favorite, and she needed things she loved, especially today, her first day of chemotherapy. She put on a pair of jean shorts and slipped into flip-flops before grabbing the tote bag with items that April had suggested. She double-checked everything. Puzzle book. *People* magazine. iPod filled with her favorite songs and earbuds. She'd grab two bottles of water from the fridge on her way out.

The doorbell rang, and she left her bedroom and walked down the hall. She put the tote bag on one of the kitchen stools and checked her watch. Mama was early. She opened the door and stared at Dez filling the door frame. "I made arrangements with the captain to go with you to your first appointment today."

"You didn't have to do that." But she was glad he had. Having him there would help calm her and bolster her spirits.

"I know, but that's what friends do."

Right. Friends. There was a time last week in Dez's car when she'd been sure he'd been feeling something more, and then again, when they'd watched that movie, but he hadn't said a word, so she hadn't, either. She ran a hand through her hair and pulled it to fall over one shoulder. "Mama will be here in a few."

"Did you eat breakfast?"

She shook her head. The thought of food made her belly jump and roll as if she stood on the deck of a ship in rough waters. "Too nervous. I'll probably regret it later." She went to the fridge and pulled out the bottles of water and put them in her tote bag. "I just don't know what to expect."

"Didn't your cancer friends have any advice?"

She raised an eyebrow at this. "Cancer friends?"

"You know what I mean."

She thought back to the dinner conversation with Page and April. "My reaction to chemo could be different than theirs," she reminded herself and explained to him.

She played with the handles of the tote bag until Dez reached over and put his hands on hers. She looked up at him, and he brought her into a hug. "It's going to be okay," he said. "I have faith in you."

Sherri brought her arms around him and let him hold her. Closing her eyes to savor this feeling, she felt as if his strength was transferring from his body to hers. They stayed entwined until a knock at the door broke them apart.

Sherri let Mama in, who didn't seem surprised to see Dez there. He leaned down to kiss Mama's cheek. "I'll have to take my own car, since I'll have to leave for work right from the hospital after Sherri's appointment."

Mama nodded, walked to Sherri and put a hand on her cheek. "Ready, *mija*?"

No, not at all. But she followed them out of her apartment. She didn't remember if she locked the apartment door, though she was sure she had. Just like she didn't remember walking down the stairs and getting into Mama's car, but they had arrived at the hospital and gone down the hall to the chemotherapy ward.

Sherri signed in on the clipboard by the nurses' station, then joined Mama and Dez in the waiting room. She flipped through one of the magazines while she waited for her name to be called, but she couldn't focus on any of the articles. Her mind raced with possibilities. Catastrophes. Fears and worries. What if she breezed through this? She might be one of those patients who handled chemo really well. Or she could be like Page and have horrible reactions to the poisons they pumped into her body. She'd lose all her hair. Lose too much weight.

What if she died?

A door opened, and a nurse in pastel yellow scrubs called Sherri's name. She rose; so, too, did Mama and Dez, and they trailed the nurse to a cubicle with a lounger attached to an IV stand. Sherri glanced at the IV bags already hanging on the stand and winced. She hated needles, though this experience had made her less fearful of them. She'd already been poked enough times to feel like a pincushion.

Sherri sat in the chair, and the nurse took

her vitals. "I'm going to give you several injections before we start the first IV."

She nodded and looked away, wincing as she felt the needle pierce her skin. Then the nurse was hooking up the IV to the port near her clavicle that the doctor had inserted earlier that week in order to protect her veins from collapsing during the course of treatment. And then the first bag started emptying into her body. She tried to distract herself with another magazine.

Dez's phone buzzed, and he glanced at it, frowning. "I don't need this. Not today."

Sherri looked up. "What is it?" she asked.

He replied, "Ras got a break in the case."

He typed into his phone, but she reached out and stopped his fingers. Sherri wanted him to stay, but she knew she needed to let him go. "You should leave."

He smirked at that. "Nice try, but I'm sticking this out with you."

"This is only the first treatment of about eight, so you can come with me to another one later." She squeezed his hand. "Mama will be here to watch over me and send you updates." She nodded toward the door. "Go."

Dez refused. "No. I promised I'd be here for you."

"What are you going to do besides watch the poisons drip into my body? I don't need you." A lie, but she couldn't keep him here. He needed to leave more than she needed him to stay.

His eyes peered into hers, and she looked away so that he couldn't see how much she wanted him to change her mind. Finally, he asked, "Are you sure?"

She pretended that the relief on his face didn't hurt. "Positive. You'll come with me on the next one."

Dez leaned in and kissed her cheek. "Text me if you need me."

She agreed, but she knew she wouldn't. He had a job to do, and while she wished that she could go with him and solve this case, he had to be given the space to do it. He texted Ras, then walked out, leaving her with Mama, who sat knitting.

Sherri flipped a few pages of the magazine on her lap, wishing she could keep her mind on the articles rather than on the man who'd just left.

DEZ MET RAS at the location he'd texted him, a parking lot of a warehouse near the Detroit River. He recognized Ras's car, a dark blue Pontiac, and parked near it. Ras stood by the pier, looking across the river to Windsor. Dez checked to make sure his gun was still holstered at his side. "You got a lead?"

Ras turned, his face grim. "I'm sorry I had to take you away from the hospital. I know how important today is."

"She understands the job." Dez glanced around the area, but didn't recognize the place. It wasn't the same warehouse they'd raided only weeks before. "What did you find out?"

"The shooter, I think."

There'd been more than one, but Dez didn't contradict him. "He knows who our leak is?"

"Maybe. Word came in this morning about a drug runner that was bragging he'd killed a federal agent during the raid." Ras consulted his notepad and pointed at the warehouse. "He works here days and probably smuggles drugs over the border at night."

"Name?"

"Omarian Jones." He handed Dez a picture that looked like a mug shot. "He's been in for possession with intent to sell."

Dez paused, remembering the name popping up in Reilly's report and that Sherri had picked up on it, as well. There had to be something behind it. "You're sure?"

"If we can trust the intel, yes." Ras squinted at the sun that beat down on them and raised a hand to shield his eyes. "I figure we go in and question Jones. See where it leads."

"As good a plan as any, I guess."

Dez checked his gun again before starting toward the warehouse. They followed the signs to the main administrative office and flashed their badges at the receptionist who greeted them. Ras gave her Jones's name, and she asked them to wait while she contacted him in the building. They heard her page him over the intercom, requesting he come to the office. Dez glanced out the window and saw a figure running across the parking lot. He tore out of the office and after the man, Ras right on his heels.

Jones darted between cars, but Dez kept an eye on his progress and narrowed the gap between them. “Running makes you look guilty, Jones!”

The man turned, gun in hand, and squeezed off a shot in his direction. A car window next to Dez shattered. Pulling his gun from the holster, Dez took cover behind an SUV and waited before moving low between cars in the direction he’d seen Jones run. It seemed Jones had gotten to the numerous shipping containers waiting on the pier.

Ras caught up to Dez, his gun drawn. “Which way?”

He pointed. “You go left. I’ll take the right.”

Ras gave a nod and moved off to the left of the closest group of containers. Dez took a deep breath and peeked around the metal container to the right, trying to locate Jones, but there was no sign of him. Dez stayed close to the container and ran down an aisle between the next two, his gun level with his face. He heard footsteps behind him and turned to see Jones standing with a gun trained on him. Dez held his hands up, but kept his gun ready just in case. "Hey, man. We just want to talk."

Jones scoffed at this and kept his gun aimed at Dez. "That's what all the cops say, but then bullets go flying."

"I'm Border Patrol investigating the shoot-out at a drug warehouse last month. You familiar?" Jones didn't answer out loud, but his face changed and Dez knew he had the right man. "Jones, let's put our guns down and talk this through."

Jones shook his head, and his finger twitched on the trigger. "I'm not stupid."

"Didn't say you were."

Dez waited for Jones to make a move, but he was stationary with his gun drawn. He was counting on Ras getting into position, since their voices were surely carried on the June breeze. A motion behind Jones confirmed this, so Dez slowly started to bend down to the ground, his eyes remaining on Jones. "I'm going to put my gun down now to show you I only want to talk. And then you lower yours, okay?"

Jones shook his head, and Dez could see

his finger twitch again as it rested on the trigger. "So your partner can shoot me? Not happening!"

Dez took a small step toward the man. "Who in your crew is talking to the feds, Jones?"

The man grimaced, his gun starting to lower an inch. "They're not stupid, either. We don't play that way."

"Someone talked. That's how we knew where to find you." Dez paused and estimated the distance between the two of them. If he could take four more steps, he'd be close enough to disarm Jones if it came to it. He took another small step forward. "Unless it was you who sold the information to the DEA. How much is the going rate for intel these days?"

The gun came up, and Jones pulled the trigger. Dez dove to the side as more gunshots filled the air. He covered his head with his arms and rolled, expecting the sudden pain of a bullet piercing his body. He'd never get the chance to tell Sherri he loved her. Never see her again. He'd break his promise of helping her through her cancer if he died.

The thought of a life without Sherri seemed impossible. Unbearable, even. He couldn't live without her. And now it seemed, he wouldn't even get that choice.

But no pain came. He saw Jones on the ground, Ras standing above him. Dez stood and grabbed his gun. He also grabbed his phone and dialed 911. He gave the details of the shoot-out, then hung up and noticed he had a text. He'd check it later.

Ras had kicked Jones's gun away from him, and the man lay in a fetal position, groaning and clutching his leg. Ras kept his gaze on Jones, but asked Dez, "You okay?"

"Thanks to you," Dez told him and meant it.

Ras gave a short nod and nudged Jones with his shoe. "You have about fifteen minutes to tell us your story before the police get here. And we have better prisons than they do."

"You shot me!" Jones shouted.

"*You* shot at my partner. Think of it as karma." Ras leaned down to Jones. "Now, who is it that's selling information?"

Jones called Ras and his mother a bunch of bad names.

Dez crouched down and cuffed Jones, then helped him to his feet. "Ambo's almost here. We can try questioning him at the hospital before we hand him over to Detroit's finest."

"And you can get back to your girl," Ras added.

Dez needed to get back to her. To tell her that he loved her, too. And that he wanted to take things to the next step. No more trying to keep up the pretense of what was normal. Because there was no normal anymore. If her cancer showed them anything, it should be that life was for living, not waiting.

Dez could hear sirens in the distance. He whispered into Jones's ear, "I bet you're our rat. You definitely smell like you took the cheese."

"I didn't tell the feds anything." Jones twisted his hands in the cuffs, insisting they were wrong about him.

"Then who did?"

Jones shook his head. "I'm not telling you. I don't have a death wish."

"But now that you're in our custody, you should feel safer to talk." Dez faced him.

A spasm in Dez's neck made him uncomfortable, and he was tempted to reach up and massage it away. Something was off. "What's going on, Jones?"

A shot rang out, hitting Jones between the eyes. Blood splattered onto Dez, and he ran for the nearest shipping container, desperate for whatever cover he could find.

Ras had his gun drawn, pointed in the direction where the shot had come from. "We've got to get out of here."

Dez moved out into the open, Ras joining him. He closed his eyes and wiped blood from his face. "This is very, very bad. A suspect dies in handcuffs while in our custody?"

Ras looked around and gestured to where the shooter had probably waited, the balcony of a nearby apartment building. "Someone shot him from above. The ballistics will clear us."

"He was in our custody when it happened, though." Dez felt sick. "This is bad."

"It could be worse."

"I thought that we finally had a break in this case. And now, we have nothing."

The ambulance pulled into the parking

lot, and Ras went to meet the paramedics and inform them of Jones's death. Dez was furious, knowing that recent events meant they weren't any closer to the truth than they had been before coming after Jones.

A police cruiser arrived. Dez knew his duty, knew he had to talk to the officers and give an accounting of what had happened. But just then, what he wanted to do most was to get back to the hospital and check on Sherri. To reassure himself that she was okay. That he still had time to tell her he loved her. To pursue a future with her. Because life without her wasn't working. That fact had been hammered home and he wanted to be near her.

He remembered the text that he'd ignored earlier and pulled out his phone. He swiped the screen to read it now and his heart sank.

Sherri was in ICU.

SHE COULD HEAR a beeping. The sound was starting to annoy her, but the effort to open her eyes required more of her than Sherri was ready to give. The cool darkness comforted her, and she wanted to stay there for a little longer. Someone held her hand and murmured prayers. Mama. Her low voice was full of beseeching words, wanting Sherri to wake up. She knew she should obey.

Her eyes flickered open, and she saw a white ceiling above her. To her left, monitors measured her heartbeat, oxygen rate and blood pressure. To her right, Mama sat, holding her hand and sobbing. Her dad stood by the window, looking out over the hospital roof.

And Dez? She moved her head from side to side slowly, to scan the room, but he wasn't there. She'd forgotten he'd been called away. But he would return. She needed him so much.

Suddenly, Mama was staring at her and she cried out as Sherri reached up and touched her mom's cheek. *"Mija!"* Mama turned to her dad. "Go tell the nurse she's awake!"

Her father hustled from the room. Sherri swallowed. Her tongue felt as if it had grown three times its normal size. "Water."

Mama clasped Sherri's hand to her chest.

"You scared us. I thought we would lose you."

"What hap...penned?"

A nurse came into the room and checked Sherri's vitals, then gave a nod to her parents. She turned back to Sherri with a soft smile. "Welcome back. How are you feeling?"

She wasn't sure how she felt. Her body seemed to have gained a hundred pounds, pushing her down into the bed, making her limbs heavy and ungainly. She swallowed a second time; even this required an effort. "Thirs...ty."

"I'll get you some ice chips after I update Dr. Frazier on your condition." She checked the levels of the IV. "I'll also get more saline to keep flushing out the chemo drugs." She looked down at Sherri. "You had an allergic reaction to one of the drugs in the cocktail and went into anaphylactic shock. They gave you epinephrine to reduce the swelling of your airways, and brought you here."

She remembered sitting in the chemo room, feeling as if she was choking. Then the room had gone black until she'd only just woken up a few minutes ago. "Dez?"

Mama stepped forward. "I texted him to let him know." Mama wouldn't let her hand go, but clung to it as if doing so would keep Sherri there with them all and not in the darkness that had claimed her earlier. "He said he'd be here as soon as he finished with the police."

"Po...lice?"

"He didn't say more."

Her dad gripped the bed rails and said in a low voice, "I don't like this, *mija*. That doctor almost killed you with that chemo."

Her mother frowned at him. "It wasn't her fault. She didn't know Sherri would react that way."

"Isn't she supposed to be there? When it's happening" He waved his hands in the air. "Who has an allergic reaction to chemo?"

"Me." Sherri winced and closed her eyes. "Go...home?"

A deeper voice answered. "They'll probably keep you overnight to make sure you're okay first."

She opened her eyes and smiled at the man standing in the doorway. "Dez."

He hurried to her side and stood next to Mama. "I came as soon as I could. I'm sorry I wasn't here."

"It's…o…kay. Here…now."

He leaned over and kissed the top of her head, and she closed her eyes, relishing the moment. Then she let herself float back into the darkness.

DURING HIS RETURN to the hospital, Dez had called the captain to let him know he'd be tied up for the rest of the day, but promised to keep in contact with Ras in case he was needed to answer more questions. He had to be in that hospital room even if all he could do was hold Sherri's hand. He turned to Perla. "What happened? She was fine when I left."

"About five minutes after they started one of the drugs, she complained about being itchy. Then her tongue swelled up, and I had to scream for the nurse to come before she stopped breathing." Perla still held Sherri's other hand. "Allergic reaction, they said. It's rare, but it's happened to other patients before."

"It's supposed to be helping her survive, but it almost kills her?" What kind of disease was this that the cure could cause just as much damage? He rubbed a thumb across the back of Sherri's hand. Combined with what happened earlier at the warehouse, this only reinforced the "life is short" theory. That he needed to share his feelings with her before it was too late. "I should have been here," he repeated.

Perla shook her head. "You couldn't have prevented anything."

He knew she spoke the truth, but his heart refused to accept it. If he'd been here, she would have been okay. He would have…

What? He wasn't a doctor. He would do anything to save her, sure, but what could he do in this situation?

He took a seat in the chair beside Sherri's hospital bed and leaned his elbows on his knees. His head in his hands, he closed his eyes and took a shuddering breath.

Perla put a hand on his shoulder. "What

matters is that you came back when she needed you."

He looked up at Perla and tried to smile, but it hurt too much. "I can't lose her. I just can't." He turned to watch the rise and fall of Sherri's chest. He stood and walked to the bed, pressed his lips against her forehead. "You have to fight this, my fierce warrior. Fight this and come back to me healthy and well." He kissed her again then pulled the blanket over her shoulders.

Perla and Horatio watched him as he ran his hand over her hair. When he turned to them, her mom whispered, "You love her." She said it as a statement, not a question.

He gave a soft nod and took Sherri's hand in his. Pressed his lips there and watched her sleep. "Always."

SHERRI WAS ALLOWED to go home that evening after rescheduling the first chemo session in two days' time. That would give Dr. Frazier a chance to adjust the cocktail to avoid the one drug that Sherri couldn't have. Lucky for her, there was an alternative that worked just as well. But the side effects were also stronger.

Sherri closed her eyes as Mama drove her to her apartment. It seemed like they'd just left the hospital before her mom shook her awake. "We're home."

Sherri blinked and looked up at the third-floor apartment. The thought of going up the stairs made her yawn. Mama noticed. "We'll take the elevator, *mija*."

Once she was in the apartment, Sherri claimed the sofa and sat down. Mama shut the front door and locked it. "Are you hungry? I can make us some dinner."

Sherri shook her head and lay down, pulling the blanket from the back of the sofa over her. "Daddy's probably waiting for you at home."

Mama put her purse and keys on the kitchen counter. "I already told him I'm spending the night here with you."

"I'll be fine." She couldn't let her mother spend more time trying to take care of her. She had to do it on her own. Had to be strong and independent. But at the moment it tired her to think of it all. She'd think of it later.

"Don't argue, *mija*. You need me after all that you went through today." Mama chose a seat on the recliner. "I came close to losing you today. If I hadn't heard you choking..." She hung her head, and tears fell from her eyes.

Sherri reached out a hand to her mother. "But I'm okay, Mama. Tired maybe, but I made it through."

Her mom raised her head, her face wet, and she reached for a tissue and wiped her eyes. "I realized today that you could be taken from me at any second. That you're so fragile. And I can't bear it. I can't lose you."

Sherri squeezed her mother's hand. "I'm not going anywhere for now, okay? I'm right here."

Mama clung to her and cried. When she'd started feeling the allergic reaction, her first thought hadn't been that she could die. She'd been thinking that she hadn't read about this in any of the literature and wondered if it was normal. Now she knew how close she'd come to a terrible outcome. And she wasn't sure how she felt about it.

Relief for surviving, of course. She also reflected on regrets for things she'd never done. Now she could understand April's bucket list. There was stuff Sherri wanted to do once she had finished treatment and was on the road to health. Experiences she wanted to enjoy. Sentiments she wanted to say.

Dez popped into her mind. Such a good man to drop everything and come to her side. She knew that he'd been knee-deep in the investigation when he'd returned. She could see the blood on his shirt, though he'd tried to hide it from her by keeping his suit jacket on. Something had definitely happened while he'd been gone, but he'd stayed by her side until the doctor cleared her to go home.

Someone who was just a friend didn't do such things. But her feelings for him went deeper, yet were unexplored in order to maintain their friendship. Maybe she would put Dez on her bucket list? Once she was healthy again.

Mama took a deep breath, then let go of Sherri's hand to grab another tissue. "I didn't want you to see me cry. We promised."

"I shouldn't have made that promise with

you. Those are real feelings, Mama. You're allowed to express them."

She blew her nose. "But I'm trying to be strong for you."

"You can be strong even when you're crying. You don't have to hide anything from me."

Mama nodded and wiped her eyes and nose. "I won't." She then stood and took another deep breath. "How does ice cream sound for dinner? I noticed when I was here before that you have a couple containers."

Sherri winced. "Well, I did before I ate them all."

Mama laughed and touched her cheek. "At least that part of you hasn't changed."

DEZ CALLED HIS team in from the field to huddle up before the start of the game. He told them who was playing what position, then put his hand in the center of the circle of teammates. They put their hands on his and shouted, "For Sherri," after counting to three.

Dez clapped his hands. "That's right. Let's show those firefighters who's the boss of this ball field." He took his spot in the dugout and made some notes on the scorecard when a shadow fell over him. He looked up into Sherri's eyes. "I didn't think you were coming tonight."

She shrugged and sat on the bench beside him. "I couldn't stay away." She pulled the sleeves of the orange hoodie down over her fingers. "Besides, I promised I'd make as many games as I could as long as I felt okay."

He noted her pallor. He bet if he took her hand in his that it would be clammy. She really shouldn't be out here after that horrible reaction yesterday. Kevin threw the first pitch. The umpire called it a strike. Sherri cupped her hands around her mouth and shouted, "That's the way, Kev. Strike him out."

He and Sherri sat silently for the first half of the inning, Dez keeping score on his clipboard while Sherri yelled encouragement to the team. When Sara caught the third out, the team ran into the dugout. Sherri fielded questions while Dez called out the batting order. "Focus, people. They aren't going to make this easy on us."

Sherri kept chatting with Sara, but Dez kept an eye on her throughout their conversation. When it was Sara's turn to bat, Dez took her spot next to Sherri on the bench. "You feeling okay?"

She groaned. "You can stop asking me that question anytime. I'm sick of answering it."

He leaned closer to her. "You don't look like you're feeling that well."

"I'm trying to forget what tomorrow is, Dez. I go back to that chemotherapy room and hope that everything turns out differently than the last time." She tugged on her hoodie sleeves so they fell past her fingers. "I need to be here so I'm distracted from my thoughts about it all. You don't know how scared I was. It was the first time I realized that this could really kill me."

He knew that more than anyone besides her parents, but he still winced at her words. "Don't talk like that."

She looked over at him. "I'm only speaking the truth."

The inning switched over. Kevin struck out the first batter, and Sherri and Dez cheered from the bench. She turned to Dez and put a hand on his arm. "Let me enjoy this game, this momentary diversion from worrying about my own problems for a couple hours."

Dez put his arm around her shoulders and pulled her to his side. He liked how feeling her body next to his made the worries and fears in his heart calm. She soothed his dark thoughts by her mere presence. "I'll distract you as much as you want." He thrust the clipboard into her hands. "You keep score tonight. That will take your mind off things."

Sherri nodded and took the pencil from his fingers to mark off the second out of the inning. "Thank you. This means a lot to me."

"I only wish I could do more for you."

"You do enough."

He only hoped that was true.

SHERRI PAUSED OUTSIDE the door of the chemo ward before putting her hand on the doorknob and turning it. She entered and walked past the chairs in the waiting room to sign in on the clipboard. Sherri, Mama and Dez all took seats in the waiting room. She took a deep breath, and Dez grabbed her hand and held on tight. "It can't be as bad as your first chemo, right? An allergic reaction wouldn't happen twice."

Her anxiety and nervousness ramped up even more. She had talked to Dr. Frazier about changing the chemo cocktail to avoid the one that had caused such a strong reaction, and she trusted her doctor. But then, she had put her faith in her for that first appointment with such disastrous results. A nurse entered the waiting room and called her name. She stood and followed her down the hall, still holding on to Dez's hand.

The room looked similar but it wasn't the same one. She took a seat on the chair attached to the IV stand. The nurse took her vitals and made notes on her chart. The nurse smiled at her warmly. "You don't have to be nervous about this. Dr. Frazier has gone over everything and will be stopping in before we start to review the changes she's made."

Sherri nodded, but didn't pay attention. Instead, she focused on her breathing. In.

Out. In. Out. Slow and easy. Anything to calm her heartbeat.

The nurse left, and a few minutes later Dr. Frazier appeared. She checked the different IV bags, then looked down at her, putting a hand on her shoulder. "I know you're nervous after what happened the last time, but this will be different."

Dez glared at the doctor. Sherri could almost feel the anger radiating from his body. "Can you guarantee that? Because she could have died," he said.

Dr. Frazier looked up at Dez and cocked her head to the side. "I understand your worries, but this should go much smoother." She crouched down so that she could look into Sherri's eyes. "They have my number just in case." She pulled the puzzle book from Sherri's tote bag and wrote her number there, as well. "Call me if you have any questions or concerns. I'm on your team throughout this process." She straightened and went to the door, turning to face her and her family. "We can get started if you're ready."

Sherri gave a nod, afraid that her voice would betray her fears. The nurse returned and gave her several injections before inserting the IV drip. She put a hand on Sherri's wrist, checking her pulse. "Do you need anything else?"

She shook her head, and the nurse left with Dr. Frazier.

Sherri looked up and watched the drip, drip, drip of the IV. She had a scratchy throat. Was that another reaction? No, she was just thirsty. She took a bottle of water from her tote bag and had a sip. Ahh, better. She looked at Dez and Mama, who were studying her intently. She shook her head. "I'm fine."

Dez let out a breath that she realized he'd been holding. "So now we wait?"

She nodded, pulled out a magazine and passed it over to him. "Need some reading material?"

He looked down at the title of the magazine and gave a chuckle. "You think I need *Cosmo* to tell me how to have a better sex life?"

Sherri glanced down at it and felt her cheeks heat. "I meant to grab *People*." She reached into her bag and pulled the right magazine out and handed it to him. "I'll take the *Cosmo*."

He raised his eyebrows at this. "You need to know how to have a better sex life?"

"It's been so long that I don't even remember how." She winced and apologized to Mama. "I forgot you were here."

Mama took the magazine from her and flipped to the article. "I think I'm the one who could use this more than the two of you. Maybe I'll get some ideas."

The blush in Sherri's cheeks deepened, and she wished that the floor would open and swallow her. Instead, she worked on a crossword. A half hour later, the nurse came in to check her vitals and change the IV bag. "Things are looking good."

Sherri massaged the back of her neck. Sitting so long in the chair made her neck, shoulders and back ache. She would like nothing more than to be able to get up and walk the hallways. Unfortunately, she still had a couple of hours before she could go home and wait for the side effects to begin. Wouldn't that be fun?

A knock on the door roused them, and

April entered the room, dressed in light blue scrubs. “I’m on my break and thought I’d check on you.”

Dez rose to his feet. “I’ll be right back.” He turned to Mama. “Do you need anything, Mrs. Lopez?”

Mama shook her head and kept knitting with the bright pink yarn. He left, and April took the seat he’d vacated. She put a hand on Sherri’s arm. “How are you feeling?”

“Better than the last time, but then, it wouldn’t take much, would it?” Sherri gave a shrug. “I don’t know. How am I supposed to feel?”

“I realize I’ve said this before, but everyone really is different. I felt fine the first day of chemo, but the next day I could barely get out of bed.” April stood and peered at her IV bags. “They have you on a strong regimen since the other one caused so many problems. That could mean either more side effects than the other one, or fewer effects but more intense.”

“Great.” She placed her puzzle book to the side. “So it’s a wait and see kind of thing. Again.”

April put her hand on Sherri's shoulder. "Welcome to the wonderful world of cancer."

CANCER SUCKED, but chemotherapy ranked almost as high on her list of things that no one should have to go through. Sherri lay on her sofa with a blanket covering her, and still the chills made her shake. She needed to get another blanket, but the thought of getting off the couch to retrieve it made her more tired than she already felt. She'd rather lay here and shiver.

Her cell phone buzzed, but she ignored it just like she had the other four calls. She couldn't talk to anyone. Didn't want to use any energy to reach out for the phone on the coffee table only inches away and answer the call, much less try to participate in a conversation.

April had warned her about this. About the strong desire to do nothing except lay inert. No sounds. No smells. No anything. Just quiet oblivion. She yanked the blanket to her chin and closed her eyes. She needed to rests for just one minute. Sixty seconds would be enough.

She woke later to a darkened room. The time on her cell phone told her it was almost midnight. Had she really slept for almost ten hours? She tested her body to see if she could find any issues. She felt less tired and less cold. She definitely didn't feel hungry; the thought of food made her stomach rebel. But she was thirsty.

She pushed the blanket off her and sat up slowly. So far, so good. She swiveled so that her feet were on the carpet then with a count of three, pushed off and stood. She waited a minute or two while the nausea settled. When she could, she walked into the kitchen, following a path from the light that glowed above the stove. She opened a cabinet and grabbed a glass, then filled it from the faucet. She drank the water quickly, then refilled the glass and sipped again.

Should she walk down the hall and sleep in her bed, or return to the sofa? She debated her options, then went to the coffee table and picked up her phone before going to her bedroom.

Her phone indicated that she had thirteen missed calls. Seven from her parents, three from Dez and the others from her brothers. She only had two voice mails, however. She sat on the edge of her bed and listened to the first. Mama wanting her to call and let her know she was okay. The second, Mama again. She didn't want to bother Sherri, but she was worried. It was late, so Sherri chose to postpone calling her back until the next day.

In the bathroom, Sherri freshened up before returning to her bed and turning on the tiny television Dez had brought over for her a few weeks ago. She flipped through the channels and landed on a repeat of a late night talk show. She pulled the covers over her and laid her head on her pillow to watch.

When she woke again, the sun streamed through her windows. She sat up, then regretted the quick movement. Her stomach couldn't handle it, and she had to take several deep breaths before the uneasiness passed. Okay, she wouldn't do that again.

She called her mom to reassure her that she was all right, but tired. After all, she'd slept most of the last twenty-four hours.

No, she didn't want her to come over. Yes, she would call if she needed her.

Then she phoned Dez back. "Ace, do you need anything?"

Was he prepared for a long list, because she could think of a lot of things she needed. "A new body?"

He laughed. "If I could do that for you, I would. But you've got to soldier through this."

She made a face, knowing he couldn't see it, but it felt better to do it. "I'd rather go through boot camp again than deal with this. At least that experience made me stronger and more confident."

"Maybe this will, too. This is just the beginning."

He didn't need to remind her of that. She ran a hand through her hair. "April said the side effects can snowball after each treatment. I'd hate to see where I'm at in three months."

"We'll celebrate once you've finished."

She smiled. "You're on."

A pause from Dez on the other end. "But seriously, do you need anything?"

She remembered April's advice that she

allow people to help her when they offered, even if it was something small. “Stephen King’s book just came out. Think you could bring me a copy?”

HE BROUGHT IT to her that night after work. Dez hadn’t even changed out of his suit and tie, but showed up with the thick volume in a plastic bag. He held it high and pumped his arm a few times as if it were a dumbbell. “I don’t know if this passes your weight restriction.”

“Funny.” She took the book from him, then cleared a space on the sofa for him. He looked so solid, so handsome. She patted the empty space next to her. “Have time to relax?”

He grimaced. “I’ve got plans with Luke tonight. But I’ll stop by tomorrow night to see how you’re doing.”

“Oh.” She tried to hide the disappointment in her voice, but knew she’d failed by the fallen look on Dez’s face. “It’s fine. I’m pretty tired anyway. Probably curl up with the book for the rest of the night.”

He leaned in and caught her gaze. “If you need me, call. Anytime.”

She nodded and stood to walk him to the door, but fatigue stopped her. He gently pressed her back down onto the sofa and pulled the blanket over her. She reached up and touched his arm. "Thank you again, Dez. Tell Luke hi from me."

He kept staring at her for a few silent moments, then he kissed her forehead and said, "You take care of yourself."

"I'm trying."

LUKE WAVED HIS hand in front of Dez's face. "Have you heard a word I said the last five minutes?"

"Honestly, I haven't been paying attention. Sorry, man." Dez threw the softball back to Luke, who caught it neatly and fired it back into Dez's glove. "Things on my mind."

"Your girlfriend?"

Dez threw the ball back to Luke. "I told you, she's just a friend."

"Yeah, yeah, I know." The ball hit his mitt, and he tossed it in the air in front of him. "She okay?"

No. She'd looked so fragile before he'd left her apartment. So vulnerable, as if it wouldn't require much to take her from him. That was what he'd been ruminating on since he'd picked up Luke at his apartment. One chemo treatment, and she looked so pale already. So sickly. It was too soon. "She started chemo, so she's having a rough time."

"That's sad."

Luke tossed the softball underhand, and Dez had to take a few steps to catch it. He examined the ball, then hurled it back to the kid. He took off his mitt. "Mind if we sit for a little?"

They moved to a bench in the park. Luke tossed the ball and caught it, then popped it up again. "Graduation is coming. Don't forget you said you'd be there."

The kid said it as if it meant little to him and even threw in a shrug. Dez knew, however, how much the kid really wanted him to show at the ceremony. "I'll be there." He glanced at Luke. "So what comes after graduation?"

The boy gave another shrug. "Mom's on my case about getting a job that pays more than minimum wage. A buddy of mine has a lead on a job with a company that supplies engine parts for the Big Three, but…" He looked down at his hands and sighed. "Is that what my life is going to become? Working in a factory eight, ten hours a day and bringing home a paycheck?" The kid said it as if it were a death sentence.

Dez punched his fist into his mitt and bent the stiff leather fingers. "It's one option. But what do you want?"

"I don't want to be stuck in a dead end for the rest of my life." Luke focused in on him. "I've been thinking about what you said about joining the marines. You were able to learn things, go places you might not otherwise, and then you got a college degree on top of that. Could I do that, too?"

Dez raised an eyebrow at this. "You're thinking of the Corps?"

Luke ducked his head. "Army, actually. My math teacher, Mr. Hicks, said I've got a mind for cryptography. Then I could study math and science in college and see where it leads." He gave a lopsided grin. "That sounds awfully good to me."

Sounded like a solid plan to Dez. The kid had potential, and he hated to see it wasted. "What does your mom say about that plan?"

"She's happy I'm graduating because it means I can work more and give her more money. But when do I get to choose what I want?"

"I'm not saying you're in a tough spot, but she's afraid of losing you." Before Luke could object, he continued. "Not your paycheck. *You.* The military isn't an easy life, but it made me the man I am and for that I'll always be grateful."

"I want the same chances. Why can't she see that?"

She probably did, but she also saw her only son drifting away from her into a harsh world. "Because she's worried that you'll get sent to war. And I'll be honest, there's always the chance that that could happen."

Luke peered at him. "But you made it through."

"By the skin of my teeth. Death came close too many times." He put a hand on Luke's shoulder. "Are there some things I wish I could unsee? Sure. Things I did that I wish could have gone differently? Absolutely. But it was worth every minute. Want me to talk to your mom? See if I can help a brother out?"

Luke nodded vigorously. "That would be great. Me and her only fight when I bring it up."

"She's your mom, so she's allowed to worry about you, your future."

"Like you're allowed to worry about your girlfriend."

Dez turned to Luke, who waggled his eyebrows and smiled, showing all his teeth. Dez ruffled the kid's hair. "You don't know when to quit."

"Sure I do. But not about this. You love her. Admit it."

"Doesn't matter what I feel, kid." He groaned and pushed off the bench. "Come on. Let's go talk to your mom about the benefits of the military."

SHERRI OPENED ONE eye and noticed that it was dark again. She did a crunch and sat up in bed. She snapped on the light on her nightstand. The digital clock read quarter past two. Great. And she was wide awake.

She really needed to get this sleeping thing under control.

She picked up the new book from the nightstand, then turned to adjust her pillows behind her back. Several strands of hair rested on the topmost pillow. She gasped and reached up to touch her scalp. Her hand came away with more strands of hair.

It was starting.

She closed her eyes, shook her head. No. Too soon. She needed to ease into this, not start by losing clumps of hair. She left the book on the bed and got up and walked across the hall to the bathroom. She leaned forward over the sink to peer into the mirror. She turned one way, then the other and noticed a lot of hair in her hairbrush. That morning she had hoped it was normal hair loss, not this. That she could somehow skip this part of the process. It didn't look as if she'd be so lucky.

She bit her lip to keep from crying. She was a strong, independent woman who didn't need hair to make her feel beautiful or special. She nodded, studying herself in the mirror. Right.

Right?

She snapped off the light and returned to her bedroom, took her cell phone off the charger and dialed his number without thinking of the time. It rang, then went to voice mail. She hung up. What was she supposed to say in a voicemail message? "I'm freaking out because I'm losing my hair?"

Well, that didn't sound too bad, but she couldn't saddle him with her problems.

Her phone buzzed. Dez. "Did you call?" His voice was gruff, still full of sleep.

"Sorry, I know it's late." She shouldn't have called. Should have waited. It wasn't as if this was an emergency that she absolutely needed him for. It was minor. Just hair.

"What's wrong? Do you need to go to the hospital?"

"What? No." She knew she was being silly. Small and petty to mourn the loss of her hair. "I wanted to talk to somebody."

She could hear his sigh come over the phone. "Good. I was afraid something bad had happened." He yawned loudly. "What's wrong?"

Something bad had happened. Would keep happening until she was left bald. She reached up, but was afraid to touch her scalp. "My hair's starting to fall out."

Silence. She wondered if he'd fallen back asleep. Then he sighed. "You knew this day was coming."

"Yes, but I didn't think it would be this traumatic." She picked up the hair from the top of her pillow. "This feels almost as bad as when I found out I had cancer."

"You're being overly dramatic, Sherri. It's only hair. You'll survive this."

She tilted her head back to lean against the bed frame. "I know. So why do I feel like bawling my eyes out?"

"Because you're going through some major stuff right now. And it's just one more thing on top of everything else." He paused. "Do you want me to come over? I'll let you cry as much as you want on my shoulder."

Tempting, very much so. But she shouldn't depend on him so much. He was a friend and partner. Things like this were reserved for family members. Boyfriends. Husbands. And yet, she knew she could trust him with this. If she asked him to, he would be there in minutes. “No, you sleep. You’re right. I’ll be fine. Sorry I woke you up.”

“You know you can call me anytime.”

She did know. And the thought made her lips smile and her heart warm.

CHAPTER NINE

SHERRI'S CHOICES FOR an outfit for the wedding had dwindled to something she could either button up or step into. And while that described her work clothes to a tee, there remained nothing that would be appropriate for Lulu's big day. She called Mama, who agreed they both needed something new for the wedding and would pick her up to go to the mall that afternoon. The thought of walking store to store made her more tired than she already was. But it was a necessary evil.

It had been four days since her second chemo appointment, and like clockwork, Sherri had noticed more clumps of hair in the tub and her hairbrush. Maybe it was time to shave it all off. She reached up and fingered the silky strands that still remained. She hated to see them go, but she would lose them no matter what she chose.

Better to do it on her terms than wait until the inevitable.

Mama picked her up, and they drove out to a megamall in the suburbs of Detroit. A beautiful sunny June day, but Sherri wore a long-sleeve top and jeans since she felt cold. She'd put on a baseball cap to disguise her thinning hair. Mama pulled into the valet parking, Sherri turned to look at her. She gave a shrug. "Why not? We deserve it."

What Sherri knew but Mama didn't say was that Sherri tired easily and wouldn't be able to walk from the parking structure to the mall in one go. She didn't protest, but let the valet open the passenger-side door for her and stepped out as if she had been born to this life. She waited while her mom got the ticket for the car. Mama placed it in her purse, then rubbed her hands together. "Where do we want to start?"

They had parked on the north side of the mall, so they began their search at the closest department store. As they walked between the cosmetic and perfume counters to get to the dresses, Sherri held her breath. The flowery fumes made her head ache and her stomach nauseous. Once in the middle of the dress racks, she took a deep breath and swallowed to keep her lunch where it belonged. Mama strolled among the racks and stopped at one, choosing a soft blue material. She pulled the dress out and placed it against Sherri. "What do you think of this one?"

Sherri glanced down and shrugged. "It's okay."

Mama put it back on the rack, and they moved closer to the center where a large rounder advertised a sale. She started to search while Sherri pushed hangers across the rack, but nothing appealed. In the past, she'd hated clothes shopping because she'd been busty, which made tops hang strangely on her frame. Now she didn't have that excuse, still, she didn't enjoy the experience.

Mama picked out a sleeveless dress in an emerald green and laid it against Sherri's body. "This is a good color on you."

Sherri took the dress and returned it to the rack. "No sleeveless. I don't want anyone to see my scars."

"The only one who'd see them would be you. I don't even notice them."

Sherri disagreed. If anything else, she would insist on this. "No sleeveless dresses."

Her mom continued looking through the racks as Sherri followed behind her as she had as a young girl and been forced to go to the mall with her parents. She gave a big sigh. "It's not going to matter what I wear anyway. Everybody'll be staring at my bald head."

Mama halted, dropped the price tag of a dress she'd been looking at and turned to face her. "Your head's not bald."

Sherri lowered the brim of her baseball cap over her forehead. "Not yet. But it's inevitable. I keep finding more hair falling out than staying in."

"Do you think it's time to shave it?"

"I don't know." She hated to give up before giving the hair that remained a chance. But for how long? "Soon, maybe."

Mama pulled out her cell phone. "I'm calling your tia Laurie to see if she can fit you in."

"*Today?* But..." She reached up to the

hair that trailed down behind her ear. She knew it was only hair. It would grow back like it had with April. Maybe it would be curly rather than flat and straight that she always had to mousse and blow-dry into waves. A full minute went by before she finally shrugged. "Okay. Let's just get it over with."

Mama spoke to Tia Laurie's receptionist and gave Sherri a nod. "She can see you at four."

Sherri glanced at her watch. It was already two thirty. "That doesn't give us much time to shop."

Mama ended the call and placed the phone back in her purse. "We have two weeks to look for a dress."

"We could have weeks before all my hair falls out."

"But do you want to wait that long?" Mama turned and pulled out a red dress with cap sleeves. "This has sleeves, and I've got a shawl from Abuela that would match."

Sherri shook her head and they went to another store and another. As they entered the fourth clothing store, she didn't care if she went naked to the wedding. Her body needed to sit down for a moment, an hour, the rest of the day. Mama turned and must have noticed because she declared it was time for a break.

After a slow journey to the food court, Sherri sat at a table as Mama bought a few things and returned with a tray that held two cookies and bottles of water. She couldn't eat any of it. The thought alone turned her stomach. "I'm not hungry. I just need to rest for a moment."

Mama broke a piece off of a cookie and popped it into her mouth. "Still feeling the ickies?"

"You could say that."

Mama opened one of the bottles of water and handed it to Sherri. "You need to stay hydrated."

Sherri nodded and took a sip. Four days after chemo and she still had a metallic taste in her mouth, but Mama was right. She needed to drink lots of water, so she guzzled the rest of the bottle. "Thank you."

Finished eating, they headed back to the valet station with Mama's purchases. She'd found a sleeveless wrap dress in coral that set off her skin tone beautifully. Sherri had found nothing, but then, her mood hadn't put her in the mind to seriously buy anything.

Mama drove them back to Detroit while Sherri closed her eyes. Mama had to shake her awake when she pulled up to Tia Laurie's salon, which wasn't far from their neighborhood.

The bell above the door announced their arrival and the receptionist smiled too brightly at them. So, she'd been told about Sherri's cancer, too. "Laurie said she needs about five more minutes before she's ready for you. Can I get you a coffee or a bottled water?"

Sherri declined and took a seat on a plastic molded chair that sat against the front window. She grabbed a magazine from the coffee table and flipped through a few pages before looking up when the bell rang again. Dez looked out of place in such a feminine salon, yet he seemed to fit in with his casual air and appreciative eye for beauty. He spotted her and chose the seat next to her. She frowned at him. "What are you doing here?"

He gave a wave to her mother, then turned to her. "I promised I'd be here, didn't I? Your mom called and said it was time."

He stared at her baseball cap and reached out to remove it. She clamped it farther on her head with both hands. "Not yet."

"In a few minutes you're going to have to take it off anyway." He touched the tip of her nose with his index finger. "It's going to be okay."

"I'm being ridiculous. I mean, it's just hair. But it's one more thing I have to give up in this fight." She hated that her eyes burned. All she wanted was to put her head against Dez's shoulder and draw strength from him.

Tia Laurie came out from the back, followed by Mama. "Sherrita, are you ready for this?"

Sherri nodded, but longed to leave the salon and go back to the car. She'd rather endure hours of shopping than this.

Dez took her hand and helped her to her

feet. He didn't let go, but led her to one of the hydraulic chairs as if she were a queen. Tia Laurie brought out a blue plastic cape and swished it over her so that it landed softly around her shoulders. She turned the chair around so that Sherri faced the mirror. "Do you want to take a picture first?"

Sherri shook her head and pulled off the baseball cap. She'd rather not have a memory of her hair so thin, patches of scalp showing through what remained. Tia Laurie sprayed her hair with water before combing it away from her face. She cut off long tresses, which fell and littered the floor by Sherri's feet. Once the hair that remained on her head was about two inches long, she turned the chair around so that Sherri couldn't see the mirror and pulled out the electric hair clippers. The snap as she turned them on made Sherri want to jump out of her skin. And the first feel of the metal blade against her scalp made her wince. A lone tear fell from her right eye and trailed down her cheek, but she didn't wipe it away. Instead, she stared straight ahead at Dez, who watched her and offered her a smile. She couldn't smile back.

Then all too soon it was over. Tia Laurie turned the chair back around and Sherri saw her bald pate. She stared at her reflection until Dez whistled. "I'm telling you, bald is sexy, Ace." Sherri laughed then let the tears flow. She covered her face and felt Dez's hands on her shoulders. "It's okay. Just let it all out."

She took a deep breath, stood and approached the mirror. She touched her image. Could that really be her? Her cheeks had thinned, making her appear gaunt. And now with a bald head, she looked like what she was: a cancer patient. Tia Laurie looked worried about her reaction. She gave a wavering smile. "Thank you, Tia. I appreciate that you took me with such short notice. It helped."

"I wish I was cutting your hair under happier circumstances, but I'm honored to have done this for you." She reached around Sherri's neck and pulled off the cape.

Mama took a seat in the hydraulic chair that Sherri had vacated. "Okay. Now my turn."

Sherri gaped at her mother, who calmly

put her purse in her lap as if she hadn't just said the impossible. "What are you doing, Mama?"

"Shave my head, too, Laurie." She looked up at Sherri. "You and Dez can't be the only ones who are sexy around here."

Sherri put her arms around Mama. "You don't have to do this. What will Daddy say?"

She gave Sherri's cheek a pat and nodded. "I told you I'd do anything to help you through this. And your father knows it's just hair. Right, *mija*? We're strong enough to know that our beauty doesn't come from the outside."

"But Mama..."

Tia Laurie cleared her throat, and she wiped at the corner of one of her eyes. "Her mind's made up."

Sherri stood back and watched as Tia Laurie repeated the cutting and shaving process on Mama. When she finished, Mama held out her cell phone to Tia Laurie. "Will you take a picture of the three of us?"

Dez stepped back and held up his hands.

"I don't need to be in any picture. Everyone knows I'm bald and sexy already."

Mama tugged at him to stand between her and Sherri. She gave a bright smile. "Say cheese, everybody."

Dez put his arms around both women and tightened his grip on Sherri. Tia Laurie took the picture, then held it out for them to see. Mama clapped her hands. "It's perfect. Now show me how to post it on Facebook."

Sherri refused. It was one thing if people saw her in person, but to post the photo on the internet for everyone to comment? "No, Mama."

"Yes. Everyone needs to see what strength looks like."

DEZ TOOK A program from the teen girl's hand, then walked into the auditorium where Luke would soon graduate. He scanned the room, trying to locate Luke's mother. He figured she must be running late since he didn't spot her amid the other parents. He took a seat in the center of a middle row and nodded to a couple who passed him to take seats next to him. The wife leaned toward him once she was seated. "You have a child graduating?"

Dez shrugged out of his suit coat and folded it over his arm since it was warm in the auditorium. "He's more like a friend. I mentored him this past year."

She gave a smile. "What's his name? Maybe I know him."

"Luke Daniels."

The woman nodded. "Our daughter is friends with him, yes. I've never met Luke, but believe me, I've heard plenty about him. Whitney said he's really changed. Probably due to your influence, then."

If Luke had changed, it was because of the kid's effort to make something better out of his life. All Dez had done was talk when he needed to and listen even more. "We mostly met and discussed homework and having goals."

"Well, it worked." She opened the program and scanned it. "Looks like he's getting an award in math and science, too."

Dez opened the program, and his jaw dropped when he saw Luke's name as one of about a dozen students receiving awards for excellence, along with their diplomas. "He never told me."

"You know teenagers."

He didn't really, but he knew Luke. If the kid had kept the news from Dez it was because he was embarrassed for some reason. He ran a finger over Luke's name. "That kid is something else." He stood and checked the room again. "I was hoping to find his mom before the ceremony started. Thought we could sit together."

But Donna never came. At least, not that Dez saw. Once the event began, he kept his focus on the stage and applauded until his hands hurt when Luke crossed the stage to receive his diploma.

After the ceremony Dez shook Whitney's parents' hands, then moved to the front of the auditorium where the graduates gathered and searched for their families. He found Luke chatting with a friend, and his face lit up when he saw Dez. They embraced. "You made it!"

"I promised, didn't I?" Dez looked around. "But I didn't see your mom. Where is she?"

Luke shrugged, and the light in his eyes

dimmed slightly. "Didn't make it. Said she had to work but she was still asleep when I left."

Dez bit back a comment. "Well, if you're free, we can go out for lunch and celebrate. On me. How does a thick, juicy steak sound?"

Luke nodded and laughed. "All right, all right. That's what I'm talking about. I'll have to call Mom's cell and tell her where I'll be."

"When we get to the restaurant." He wasn't going to give Donna the chance to take away anything from this moment. Dez put his arm around Luke's neck and dragged him away from the other students. "I'm so proud of you. And what's this about an award for math and science?"

Luke shrugged. "It's no big deal. I took a test and scored high is all."

"That's all? That's more than I accomplished when I was your age." He'd barely passed any class but phys ed. And he'd never scored high on any tests. The kid really didn't know how special he was.

They headed for the lot where Dez had parked. He paid the attendant, and they drove to a steak house that was packed with the after-church crowd. Luke winced. "How long of a wait is this going to be?"

"Doesn't matter. It's not every day you graduate high school." Dez put their names in with the hostess and they lounged in the entrance. Luke paced and bounced up and down until Dez turned and looked at him. "Is there something you want to tell me? You fidget when you're keeping a secret. It's one of your tells."

"The real reason Mom didn't come to the graduation ceremony…she…" He cracked his knuckles. "I joined the army and she's angry with me. We argued, both said some things." He glanced over at Dez. "Are you disappointed in me, too?"

Dez gaped at the kid. "Disappointed? No. Proud as hell, man. I'm impressed. Why didn't you tell me when you enlisted? I could have gone with you."

"I had to do it on my own. To prove to myself that I was a man making my own choice, you know?" He let out a big sigh. "But Mom doesn't get it."

"She'll come around."

"Well, she's got less than a month. I leave

in the middle of July for basic training." He gave a grin. "I scored off the charts on the ASVAB in several areas and had my choice of several positions, but I chose linguistic cryptology."

Dez gave a low whistle. "Code breaking."

Luke beamed. "They're going to teach me languages and codes and all this stuff I had no idea existed. My recruiter, Sergeant Listo, said I was in good shape, but recommended working out to build muscle before I go. You think we could start doing that instead on our nights together?"

"You bet. I'll get you a guest pass for my gym and we can go together until you leave." Dez put his hand on Luke's shoulder. "You saw something you wanted and you worked toward that goal. You achieved that and now you've made a new one. You're becoming a real man."

"Being a man is making and achieving goals?"

"Part of it. Some of it is also providing for your loved ones. And you've been doing that since you could collect bottles and cans to turn in for money." Dez pulled him into a crushing hug. "Soooo proud of you."

Luke protested and pushed away from him. "Don't get all mushy on me," he insisted. But the kid was all smiles as he said it.

DEZ DREADED THIS softball game against the Detroit Cop Union, their archrivals. Dez gathered the team around him before the first pitch. "Sherri's feeling sick and won't be here tonight, so let's win this one for her." He put a hand in the center and everyone placed theirs on top. "Victory on three. One, two, three."

"Victory!"

They were first up, so Dez yelled out the batting order and handed the score sheet to Luke. "Thanks for keeping score since she couldn't make it."

"Who couldn't make it?"

Dez jerked his head up and spied Sherri in the entrance of the dugout. She wore a baseball cap over her bald head.

He put his hands on his hips. "Does nothing keep you down? You're supposed to be home resting."

"I feel fine." She stepped forward.

He noticed the dark circles under eyes set in a pale face. If that was fine, he'd eat his mitt. She sat next to Luke on the bench, but didn't take the score sheet from him. Several of the team greeted her, touching her in the process.

Dez wanted to put a barrier around her to keep any of their germs off her, to protect her from more harm than the cancer already posed. Instead, he went to the chain-link fence that divided the dugout from the ball field.

She joined him not long after, yelling out encouragement to the batter. Then she turned to him. "Don't be angry with me. I wanted to be here."

He could understand her desire to see the team and be around people, but it could cost her more than it might help her. "It's too much of a risk. You could catch something and get sicker than you are."

"I told you I'm fine."

He scowled even more as he faced her. "Tell that to someone who believes that. You don't look fine."

She gave a soft smile. "You really know how to charm a girl."

"I'm not trying to charm you. I want you to be safe and get healthy. Showing up tonight is not doing either one of those things."

She looked down at her hands. "I needed to get out of the house."

"So go to your mom's."

"How is that any different than coming here? I'm outside in the fresh air and surrounded by friends. That sounds like a good idea to me."

He ignored her, turning his focus back to the game. He stood and put his fingers through the chain-link fence that separated them from the infield. The batter got a hit and ran to first base. Safe. Dez clapped and cupped his hands around his mouth. "All right, Sara. That's showing them."

Sherri put a hand on his shoulder. "It's not like I'm asking you to put me in the game. I'm just sitting on the bench."

"Then go do it." He knew that this anger would only put a wedge between them, but he didn't know how to let it go. He'd die for this woman, he'd trade places with her if he could, but she didn't get it. Didn't understand that she needed to do her part if he couldn't fix it for her. She needed to follow doctor's orders and do everything necessary to get healthy again. Hanging out at a softball game didn't fit the bill.

She made a small noise of protest or disgust, he wasn't sure which, and sat next to Luke again.

The game ended with a double play by his team that left the opponent's tying run on third base. The teams gathered and formed two lines, then walked, slapping hands and muttering, "Good game."

Dez stayed around to pick up equipment. Sherri left the dugout and went to second base to get it and return it to him. When she put it in the large duffel bag, she looked up at him. "I wish you could understand what I'm going through. That you could see how important being here tonight was for me."

He shoved the other bases into the bag and stared at her hard. "So help me understand."

"I know the risks of going out in public when my immune system is shaky at best, but I need to be with people sometimes. I need to feel like I'm still included with everyone and not as if I'm quarantined. And alone. I don't want to feel like my life is over because I'm dealing with this and can't do the stuff I used to do." She wiped the corner of her eye and looked away. "I need to feel normal again."

"But what if you get sick?"

"I'm already sick!" She dropped the volume of her voice. "But I'm not dead. At least not yet."

She strode off then, leaving him with Luke. Together they collected the rest of the equipment. Luke whistled. "You really know how to tick her off."

Dez watched her retreating figure as she walked through the parking lot. "That's not what I was trying to do. I want to protect her."

"By trying to protect her you made her feel like she didn't belong here. And that's what she wanted tonight. To belong. But then, I'm a kid, what do I know?" Luke shrugged and ran to the row of bats leaning against the chain-link fence.

Dez continued to stare out at the parking lot. He hadn't been wrong in wanting to keep her safe. All he wanted was for her to be whole again.

Come to think of it, maybe that was what she wanted, too.

AFTER HER ARGUMENT with Dez, she hadn't heard from him, even though it'd been a few days. Trying to put aside his absence, she invited April and Page over for a girls' night. But when the night arrived, only April showed at her apartment. "Page wanted to come, but she's not doing so good right now."

"Problems with her radiation?"

"She didn't have enough energy to get dressed when I showed up at her condo. She just wanted quiet." April grimaced. "The treatment's really taking a toll on her this time."

They made virgin cocktails since Sherri had to abstain from alcohol while she was in chemo. But they drowned big bowls of popcorn with melted butter before taking seats on the sofa and watching a chick flick. April painted her toenails as the first one started. She glanced over at Sherri. "You should come with us to the Hope Center. They're great at helping you get through this."

April had invited her before, but the idea of being with a big group of strangers who were sick like her didn't appeal. "I'm not sure."

"It sounds like a bunch of hooey, but sharing what I'm going through with other women has really helped me." She put the cap back on the nail polish and peered at Sherri. "So how is chemo going?"

Sherri shrugged. "Fine."

April narrowed her eyes. "How is it really going? Truth this time."

That was the big question, wasn't it? "I don't know. One minute I think I'm going to be okay, then the next I'm freaking out about losing my hair. I just want to feel normal again. How long do I have to feel like there's an alien inside my body? Some being that's invaded so that I don't even recognize it anymore?"

"It'll take some time, but you will feel like yourself one day. Promise." April started to apply another coat of nail polish to her toes.

"Right now I don't see how that's possible." Sherri rubbed her shoulder, then paused the movie. She turned to face April fully. "Three months? Six? A year? How long?"

"It depends on the person." When Sherri sighed, April held up her hand. "Everyone's journey with this disease is unique. That's why the Hope Center helped me. I could hear others tell their stories. Some were the same, some not." She recapped the nail polish. "For me, personally? I didn't feel normal for the first six months, and even now, I still have days when I feel like you do. The thing is, it's not about going back to how you felt before the cancer. It's about learning to live with a new normal. Once you can accept that, things will get better. You won't keep comparing your before cancer self to after. You'll just..." April gave a shrug. "Just be." She laughed. "Page calls all this my mumbo jumbo. I don't know. Maybe it is. But it's what gets me get through the day."

Sherri considered this and nodded. "What is it like where you are on this journey?"

"I'm nearing the end and it terrifies me." She smiled at this. "It doesn't make any sense, does it? I should be relieved. And don't get me wrong, I am. But I'm scared that the rest of my life starts now and I have no more answers than before. Just a sense that I need to make it count."

"That actually sounds pretty wise to me."

April laughed again, but wiped at the tears in her eyes. "We're supposed to be having a girls' night, not crying about how much cancer took from us." She raised her virgin cocktail. "Here's to finding purpose in the darkest moment."

"To feeling normal."

THE DOORBELL RANG, and Sherri hurried to answer it, expecting to find Dez standing on her doorstep, apology in hand. Instead, her cousin Mateo was leaning on the door frame, carrying a plastic bag. "Hey."

She looked behind him, but he was alone. "Did Dez send you?"

He shook his head and entered the apartment. "No, I wanted to see how you were feeling. Do you need anything?"

"No. Today is a good day." And it really had been. She'd had more energy than the day before. Enough to go through her closet and get things organized for her return to work in the next couple of weeks.

"Great."

He kept looking past her, but eventually, glanced up at the top of her bald head. She reached up to rub it. "I had to shave it because it kept falling out."

"My mom refused to shave her head. Said it meant she was giving up. Not that you have, but..." He picked at a spot on his sleeve. "Sorry, cuz. Seeing you like this brings up a lot of bad memories for me."

"Is that why you stopped by? To remember the bad times?"

"No." He finally looked up at her straight on and sighed. "I've been avoiding you, and Lulu said that it wasn't being fair to you. It's not your fault you got the same cancer that killed our mom."

She remembered how Tia Connie had been sick for so long. Years, it seemed, but Sherri had been a teenager and things like time had a different definition then. "So you're here because Lulu yelled at you?"

"She can be really persuasive." He held up the plastic bag. "I brought you one of those adult coloring books and some crayons. Thought it might be calming or something."

She took the bag from him. "Thank you. I'll have to give it a try." She motioned to the sofa. "Do you want to sit down?"

He seemed uncomfortable at the thought of having to be here any longer than he needed to. "I can't stay. I have to meet a client to go over some testimony." He took a step toward her, then pulled her into an awkward hug. "Please take care of yourself."

"I'm trying."

He patted her softly then let go. "Will you be at Lulu's wedding?" he asked.

"Planning on it. Assuming I can find something to wear. And you know… If I'm feeling okay."

"Right." He walked to the front door, then turned around abruptly and pulled her into a genuine hug. "Fight this with all you've got, okay? I can't lose anyone else to this horrible disease." He kissed her cheek.

She nodded, and he left the apartment.

Mateo's visit had felt off, but then, she knew a lot of it had been his discomfort with her cancer. She did the math and realized that Tia Connie had only been five years older than she was now. Too young to lose so much. Lulu had to be remembering her mom as she prepared to get married. Tia Connie had wanted to live and be there for her baby girl just as Sherri wanted to fight this and see another day.

She found her knees growing weak and pulled a kitchen stool from the counter to support herself. Tia Connie had wanted to fight, but had lost her life all the same. Would Sherri be like her? Or would she have the odds in her favor and beat this thing?

Did it come down to luck? To science? Or to faith? If she believed she'd survive, then she would? She rested her elbows on the counter and buried her face in her hands. She didn't know, couldn't know, what would happen. Raising her head, she did know that she wouldn't give up without a fight.

SHERRI CHECKED HER tote bag for the fourth time to make sure she had everything she needed for her chemotherapy visit. Magazines, check. Romance novel, check. Snacks… She pawed through the bag and frowned. She was sure she'd put in a small bag of hard candies, but she couldn't find them. In her kitchen, she started opening and closing cupboards. She found a bag of pretzels and a half-eaten package of crackers, but no candies.

A knock on the door distracted her from her search. She opened the door to find her brother Hugo standing there. She glanced behind him. "Where's Mama?"

"Hello to you, too." He pushed past her and stepped forward. "I told her I'd take you to your appointment today." He narrowed his eyes at her. "You have a problem with that?"

"Is she feeling okay?" Maybe Sherri should call her and check up on her. It wasn't like Mama to promise to do something and then not show up.

"She's fine, but I wanted to take you instead."

She watched him for a moment. "Why didn't she call me to tell me she wasn't coming today?"

"Listen, don't make me regret volunteering. What? Only Mama can take you to the hospital? None of the rest of us are allowed to help?" He put his hands on his hips. "Can't I do something nice for you once in a while?"

"I didn't mean it like that." She gathered her tote bag and put it over her shoulder. Hugo took it from her and carried it himself. "I'm not too weak to carry that," she told him.

"Shut up and let me do it."

She checked that she had everything she needed for the appointment before leaving the apartment and following her little brother to his car. He opened the door for her and waited for her to get in before slamming the door shut. He'd never done that before. She frowned at him as he entered the car on the driver's side. "I'm not dying, Hugo." He swore softly, at which she smacked him in the shoulder. "Better not let Mama hear you talk like that."

He started the ignition and gunned the engine. "We haven't hung out in a while, so I told Mama I'd take you for once and let her have a day off."

"So you keep saying."

He sighed. "Why do I have to have an ulterior motive?"

"Because you're my little brother, and I know you better than you know yourself." She snapped her seat belt into place as he sped to the hospital. "We have plenty of time until my appointment. You don't have to break land speed records to get there."

"Ha-ha." But he immediately eased off the accelerator. "Actually, I figured since we're going to have a few hours to bond that you could give me some advice."

"And you couldn't simply call me instead? Please don't tell me it's problems with your nonexistent girlfriend." She shook her head.

Hugo scowled at her. "Forget it. We can just sit in silence while the doctor poisons you."

No one spoke until they reached the hospital. Hugo parked, then ran around to help her out of the car. She batted away his hand when he grabbed her arm to help her stand. "You can stop doing that. I'm perfectly capable of getting out of a car." She took the tote bag off his shoulder. "And I can carry my own bag, thanks."

"You sure don't like people helping you, do you?"

She began walking to the hospital. "I don't like people assuming I can't do something. Yes, I have cancer, but I'm not helpless."

"Would never accuse you of that," he muttered behind her as he followed her into the building.

Once the injections had been given and the IV started, Hugo looked at her, his face white. She smirked. "Don't like needles?"

He gave a shudder and winced. "You never did."

She shrugged. "I'm used to them now." She pulled out a book of puzzles and handed it and a mechanical pencil to her brother. "Here. It will help pass the time."

Hugo accepted the items and opened the book to a random page. He started a puzzle, then quit after a minute. "I'm serious about needing advice."

Sherri wrinkled her nose. "It's not about girls, is it?"

"I do fine with the ladies." He shook

his head. "No, this is about my career." He frowned. "Or lack thereof."

"Ooo, college graduate, you scored points for using that word correctly."

Hugo waved the puzzle book at her. "Never mind."

Sherri put her magazine down and put her hand over his hand. "All right, I'll knock off on the sarcasm. It just comes naturally to me when I'm talking to you. It's all part of being the big sister, you know."

He smiled. "It's part of being the baby brother, too."

She folded her hands in her lap. "So, what advice are you looking for?"

"I graduated over a month ago and I've only been on two job interviews. One was perfect for me, but I didn't get a call back. The second had nothing to do with my degree and would have been a waste of time."

"Could it have led to something bigger?"

"Maybe, but I need more than possibilities. I'm tired of living with Mommy and Daddy and working a minimum wage job while I look for something else." He doodled on the puzzle page. "How did you find your job?"

The question surprised her. She hadn't pictured Hugo as an adult before. He would always be her baby brother even when they were both in their eighties. "I thought you wanted to go into business. You want to work for Border Patrol?"

He looked up at her. "They don't need accounting and finance majors, do they?"

"Not unless you have a background in the military or police." She remembered being where Hugo was after she'd finished her time in the army. She'd gotten her college degree, then spent three months searching for a job in a market that was glutted with qualified applicants. "I contacted a job recruiter who helped me with my résumé, my interview skills, all of that. I let all the aunties and uncles know I was looking for a job and used all those contacts. It was Tio Roberto who had a buddy that knew someone in the Border Patrol office and said they had openings. But it came at the right time and it was the right fit. You can't force it."

He groaned. "You know I'm not good at the waiting thing."

Did she ever. He was the one who had

snooped to find their Christmas presents before the actual day, then woke everyone up at four in the morning to open gifts. He really wasn't good at the waiting thing.

"Let everyone know you're looking for a job and what you want. Check out the job recruiter's office by Tia Laurie's beauty shop. And keep working where you are until a smart offer comes along."

"You don't give easy answers."

She motioned to the IV stand. "I'm not exactly in an easy situation myself. The thing is, you have to learn the lessons in the position you are now, before you move on."

He glanced at the tubes connected to her and winced. "And what lessons are you learning?"

Good question. If April was here, she'd cross off a grocery list of things she'd gained by fighting cancer. She pushed herself to answer. "That I'm stronger than I thought I was. That what I thought was important has changed. And that my bald head, the nausea, all of it, is temporary. I need to get through this and I'll find answers on the other side."

Hugo considered this, then nodded. “I really hope you kick this cancer in the butt, sis.”

She gave him a smile and squeezed his hand. “I’m doing my best.”

CHAPTER TEN

THE MORNING OF the wedding, Sherri lay on the bathroom floor next to the toilet and wished for a different body. She'd had her fourth chemo appointment two days before, so she was right on schedule with the nausea and vomiting.

She pulled her phone from her hoodie pocket and dialed Dez's number. The call went straight to voice mail. He must be either with Luke or working out. She waited for the beep, then took a deep breath. "Dez, it's me. I'm not going to make the wedding. I hate to miss it, but I'm too sick. I'll call you later. Thanks."

She pressed End Call on the phone's screen and stared at the ceiling, debating about whether it needed a fresh coat of paint. She'd heard from Page that the effects of chemo would snowball after each treatment, but she hadn't expected to feel this horrible. She grabbed her phone and started scrolling through the contacts to find Lulu's name when it started to ring. Dez. "I'm sorry to cancel last minute."

"You're not canceling."

"Dez, I'm lying on the bathroom floor because I can't risk being any farther away from the toilet. I'm really sick this time."

"How much of it is chemo and how much is nerves about facing your family?"

She put a wrist over her eyes, which ached from the bright sunlight coming in from the window. "It's the chemo."

"Sure about that? I didn't figure you for a coward."

She sat up and rested her back against the bathroom door. "I'm no coward."

"So eat some crackers and drink ginger ale, and I'll pick you up at three like we planned."

This from the man who had gotten angry when she'd shown up to hang with her friends at a ball game. She couldn't just wish this nausea away like it was a mental thing. The thought of the smell of flowers, the loud music and all the people at the wedding made her sweat and shake. "You don't get it. I can't go."

"Let's be honest. You won't go. There's a difference."

She sighed and put the phone to her forehead. The man was insufferable. He never listened to her and always assumed the worst of her. Right? Or did he want to push her when she was unable to motivate herself? She put her phone back to her ear. "Come over at three, but I'm not going. We can stay here and watch movies or something."

"Nice try. Take a shower and put on that dress you bought. Be ready when I get there."

He hung up before she could. She tapped on her phone, took a deep breath then released it. He might be maddening, but he was right. She had to do this. If nothing but to prove to Dez that she could.

AT A FEW minutes before three, Dez knocked on Sherri's apartment door and wondered which version of her would answer. The dressed up and ready to go one? Or the defeated and given up one? The door opened and he whistled at the vision before him. "You look smashing."

She gave a weak smile and reached up to the floral scarf she'd tied around her head. She looked him up and down, her smile widening. "You don't look too bad yourself."

Despite the green tinge about her complexion, she really did look great. The yellow lace dress made it seem like she was alive and vibrant. "I'm serious."

She reached up and touched the knot of his tie. "So am I."

He put his hand on her bare arm, wanting, no, needing, to touch her. She was a goddess. He only wished she could be his.

He took a few steps inside the apartment and looked around. Dirty dishes cluttered the kitchen sink. A blanket and pillow sat on the sofa as if she'd just risen from it. She followed his gaze and shrugged. "I didn't move much from the sofa the last couple of days."

He peered into her eyes and could see the war between fatigue and determination being fought there. "We don't have to go. You're right. We can stay in and watch a movie or two."

She looked down at her dress. "I got ready for this wedding. We're going."

"You're not well. I was wrong to push."

He should have realized that she was telling the truth about her health. Why hadn't he listened when she'd tried telling him earlier? Because he figured that he knew better than she did. He should've kept his mouth shut.

"I'll be fine. I've got crackers in my purse just in case." She held it up for him to see. "Let's go."

"I was wrong."

"Wait. Should I write this day on the calendar? Dez actually admitted that he was wrong?" She gave a chuckle. "No, you were right. Nerves about seeing my family were making this harder for me than they should be. I'll be fine once we get there. You'll see."

He touched her cheek tenderly. "Do you know how amazing you are?"

She pulled his hand away from her face. "Don't make me more than I am. I'm just me."

That was what made her amazing. She was so brave, so beautiful, but she didn't see it. He turned and opened the front door for her. She passed by him, and he caught a whiff of something that smelled like honey, a scent that could only be Sherri. He paused as she locked the door, then held her elbow as they took the stairs down so she wouldn't trip wearing impossibly high heels and a long flowing dress. At his car, he opened the passenger-side door for her, then closed it and ran around to get in on the driver's side, not wanting to keep her waiting for too long.

He drove them to an old church in downtown Detroit and noticed that the parking lot was full. Cars lined the surrounding streets. He pulled his car back in front of the church to let Sherri out before searching for an open spot to park.

By the time he reached her, Perla and Horatio had joined her along with her youngest brother, Hugo. He adjusted his tie and navy suit coat. Perla looked him up and down and nodded. "You'll do."

He turned to Sherri, a question on his face. She waved a hand. "An ex-boyfriend is in the wedding party, a friend of the groom's, I guess. Mama wants to make sure he regrets letting me go."

The thought of an ex-boyfriend made him want to go on the warpath to protect his goddess warrior. But he squelched the urge and clasped his hands in front of him. "How long ago was this? You haven't dated anyone since Dave, and that was three years ago."

Her expression was incredulous. "You remember Dave?"

Hugo nodded somberly. "We all remember him. Mama thought you were going to end up married to that jerk."

"He wasn't a jerk. He just had other priorities that didn't include me." Sherri explained to Dez, "I dated Jason off and on in high school and some of college."

Mama reached over and straightened Dez's tie. "Never mind, *mija*, you've got Dez here to make him jealous."

"Jason's married with kids, Mama. He's moved on. Trust me." Sherri put her elbow in the crook of Dez's arm. "Can you please take me inside? I need to sit down. This heat is getting to me."

Thoughts of witty comebacks or disparaging comments about ex-boyfriends fled at the request and he led her into the church. Her cousin Mateo met them at the sanctuary door. His eyes ran over Sherri from the scarf covering her head to the lace dress that covered more of her chest than showed. He cleared his throat. "You look...um, good, cuz."

Sherri shook her head. "Don't mince words, I know I look terrible."

Dez put his hand on hers. "You're beautiful, Ace. Don't listen to him."

Mateo motioned to the left since they belonged to the bride's family. They took seats about two rows from the back at Sherri's insistence. "Just in case I need to get up real quick," she whispered in his ear.

Her parents sat closer to the front where most of the family had congregated as they waited for the ceremony to begin. Sherri tugged at her head scarf. "I hate this thing. It itches."

He looked at it and wrinkled his nose. The silk floral scarf was fussy and didn't seem to match Sherri's sense of style. She was more classic and simple. She made the statement, rather than the clothes she wore. "So take it off."

"You saw Mateo's reaction. It's better if I stay covered."

"What are you more worried about? Their comfort or yours?" He reached up and pulled the knot at the back of the scarf until it loosened and sat in his hand. He placed it in her lap. "There. You're gorgeous."

She tentatively touched her bald head. "You think it's okay?"

He kissed the top of her head. "It's perfect."

Some of Sherri's family stopped to say hi, then continued down the aisle to sit near the front. He nudged her. "See? They didn't gawk or stare."

She let a smile tease her lips before throwing the scarf around her neck in a casual loop. Dez put his arm across the back of the pew, waiting for the ceremony to start.

THE YACHT CLUB off the Detroit River hosted the large wedding reception. Dez used the valet parking, saying he wanted to make sure his car was secure. Sherri really knew that it was because of her, so she wouldn't have too far to walk. He needed to get over this idea of her fragility. She had always been made of tough stuff and cancer couldn't change that.

Lulu had placed them at a table in the middle of her family so that everyone got a good view of her and her bald head. Okay, so maybe that wasn't the reason why they were surrounded by well-meaning relatives, but it felt as if a spotlight shone down on her and beckoned every family member to stop by and ask how she felt. Sherri thought about going into the restroom and putting the scarf back on, but her head felt better without it. Luckily, the bridal party arrived and captured everyone's attention. The party had officially begun.

Sherri picked at her dinner for a while before offering it to Dez, who ate it with relish. She wanted cake anyway, and baked chicken would only crowd her stomach. Then it was time for dancing, the part she always loved at weddings. Sure, the ceremony had been beautiful and the wedding toasts touching. But the beat of the music thrummed through her veins with the need to move. She asked Dez, "Want to dance?"

He looked over at the empty dance floor. "Don't the bride and groom have to go first?"

"They already did. You were eating your fourth piece of cake."

He grinned at her. "Third."

"Whatever. Now it's our turn." She stood and held out her hand. He sighed, wiped his mouth with a napkin, then followed her to the dance floor. They fell into the fast rhythm of the salsa. He twirled her and moved them around the floor. Dez might have been tall and solid, but he had agility and grace that most wouldn't suspect. The music permeated the air with a rhythm that pushed them apart, then pulled them together. They held each other; they moved away. The song ended with her in his arms, him standing behind her and her hand on his cheek. Being there, like that, felt natural.

Her heart beat quickly, and her breath came in loud gasps. He started to lead her off the dance floor, but the music changed to a soft ballad. She pulled him into her arms and their bodies started to move. He held them close, his hand on the part of her dress that opened to her bare back. The heat of his hand traveled up and down her spine. She leaned forward to rest her head on his shoulder, and she could feel his breath on the back of her neck. Savoring this moment, she closed her eyes and followed his lead around the dance floor.

He swallowed and she could feel the movement of his jaw. He backed away so that she had to raise her head to look at him. He licked his lips and looked down into her eyes. "Sherri, there's something I've been wanting to tell you."

She put a finger to his mouth. “Shh. Don’t say anything. I love this song.”

He gave a soft smile, then dipped her and brought her back up to meet him. They danced two more songs after that, then she had to beg off and return to their table. He waited until she sat down before he glanced at the bar. “I’ll go get us some ice water.”

Sherri fanned her face and nodded. “Thanks, Dez.”

As he left, Mateo took his seat. “What’s the deal with you two?”

“There is no deal. How many times do we have to say we’re friends?” Dez was a close confidant, her partner. That didn’t make a deal of any sort.

Mateo raised one eyebrow. “You sure you want to stick to that story after the entire family watched you two on the dance floor?”

She looked down at her hands, feeling the heat in her cheeks. “It was just a dance.”

“More like four.”

She jerked her head up to face her cousin. “You don’t know what you’re talking about. We’re good friends and good partners. Nothing more.”

"You might want to check with him because I think things have changed. At least, for him." Mateo stood and put a gentle hand on her shoulder. "Let me know if you need anything, cuz. I'm always here for you."

He nodded to Dez as he returned with two large glasses of water. Dez handed one to Sherri, who gulped about half of the contents before he had a chance to take a seat. "Thank you. I really needed that."

"Me, too." He took a sip of his, then watched the people on the dance floor for a moment. "When you're ready to go up there again, let me know. We could show some moves to this crowd."

They'd already shown more than she'd realized if Mateo was right. "I don't know. I'm pretty tired."

"If you want to leave, I can bring the car around." He reached out and touched her arm, and the heat from his hand seemed to scorch her skin. "You know I'd do anything you want."

That was the problem.

Things had changed since she'd been diagnosed with cancer, and she hated it. She wanted everything to be like it was before, including her relationship with Dez. But the look in his eyes tonight showed that it couldn't be the same. Wouldn't be. If he wasn't being overprotective of her, he looked at her with pity…and something else she was afraid to explore.

That thought gave her a lump in her throat that she couldn't swallow away. As much as she might want something more with Dez, now was not the time for that. Later, when she was better. Maybe. When she could think about something more than just getting through the day. Then they could talk about it. But not now.

She just had to convince him of that.

SHE'D NEVER LOOKED more beautiful. Sure, her bald head made her eyes look huge in her face, but gorgeous nonetheless. Her beauty came more from within. Sweet, kind, but hard in places she needed to be. Fiery with passion. Protective of family and friends.

She was perfect. And perfect for him, if only he could convince her to see it.

He adjusted the shawl around her shoulders, and she turned to smile at him. Felt like an arrow to his heart. He was hopeless before her.

He put a hand on her shoulder. "Sherri…"

She yawned then and waved away his concern. "I guess I am ready to go. I'll start saying goodbyes. With all my family here, it will probably take an hour before we can get out of here." But she didn't sound resentful of that fact, only proud.

He watched her walk away to the table where her uncle Rico sat talking to her parents. She gave everyone hugs and laughed at something her uncle said. Then the bride, Lulu, stopped by, and more hugs and laughs. He watched her progress though the reception hall as she gave her leave.

"She's special."

Dez turned and saw Mateo watching her, as well. He nodded. "She is."

Mateo narrowed his eyes at him. "Don't hurt her or you'll answer to me."

"I would never hurt her. I love her too much."

"So that's how it is?"

Dez nodded and grabbed Sherri's purse from the table. Mateo whistled. "Does she know?"

"Not yet." He'd hoped the moment had been right earlier, but she'd silenced him. He couldn't be quiet much longer.

"Be sure you know what you want from her before you say anything."

"I will." He shook Mateo's hand. "We should get breakfast next week. I'll update you on Luke."

Mateo gave a nod at the name. "Has he decided what he wants to do after graduation?"

"He leaves for the army soon."

Mateo smirked at him. "Well, it worked for some."

Sherri joined the two of them. She smiled at Mateo. "Now that Lulu is married, when will it be your turn?"

He rolled his eyes. "You're worse than the aunties. I'm fine on my own."

She took her purse from Dez. "My guess is that they already have someone lined up for you."

Mateo kissed her cheek. "And what about you?"

She raised an eyebrow at this. "They know better than to mess with me."

"Right." He gave her a quick, careful hug.

"Good luck with that." He shook Dez's hand once more. "You two have a good night. And remember what I said."

When Sherri seemed confused about that, Dez led her out of the ballroom and down the stairs to the valet stand. "What was that?" she asked.

He shook off her question and handed his ticket to the valet. "Are you feeling okay?"

She looked up at him, frowning. "I'll be better after I get some sleep. But I'm okay."

The valet returned with his car, and Dez opened the passenger-side door for her. She folded her long legs inside, and he shut the door and walked around to the driver's side, tipping the valet. He got inside the car and started driving toward her apartment. Her scent floated in the air between them, honey and something that was uniquely her. Intoxicating.

They didn't talk on the drive home or as they walked up to her apartment. She unlocked the door and turned to face him. "Thank you for going with me tonight. I couldn't have done this on my own."

"You don't have to be alone."

She gave a smile that didn't quite meet her eyes. "Are you volunteering?"

He took a step closer to her so that she had to tip her head back to look at him. "What if I was?" He touched her cheek, then the curve of her top lip.

Her lips parted as she took a step back. "Dez, what are you doing?"

It was now or never. "Something I've wanted to do for a long time."

He pulled her into his arms, reveled in the taste of her, the feel of her. Then she was kissing him back, and the sweetness made him think of a fine wine.

Suddenly, she quit kissing him and pushed away. "We have to stop."

His chest ached with instant disappointment. "Why?"

She shook her head. "I can't do this."

He stepped forward and cupped her cheek. "Why not? We're friends. Best friends."

The tip of her tongue flitted out of her mouth and wet her top lip. "I'm going back to work next week and we can't be partners again if we pursue this. The captain would reassign us. Is that what you want?"

He knew she was being sensible, but the

last thing he wanted in this moment was to be reasonable. He wanted to be reckless and tell her he loved her. To pursue a different future with her. "Would that be such a bad thing?"

"Just so we can feel our oats or whatever this is? Yes. I don't trust anyone in that office more than you. And if we risk what we already have for something more, when there's no guarantee that it will work out, then we'll have really lost something special. That doesn't make any sense." She crossed her arms over her chest. "I'm sorry, Dez, but I can't agree to that right now."

"But don't you feel the electricity between us? The way we fit together when we danced? Or when you kissed me back? That doesn't come around every day."

She took a small step back. "The wedding is making you think things that you wouldn't normally."

He gripped her by the shoulders, willing her to understand. "What's making me think is you. I've loved you since I met you and you love me, too."

"Of course I love you." His heart soared, but she sidestepped his embrace and went inside the apartment. "But as a friend. I can't offer you anything more."

Oh.

His hopes fell and lay on the floor at his feet. She was giving him the "let's just be friends" speech? Maybe everything he'd been feeling had been one-sided. Maybe the intimacy that sprang up between them as they danced hadn't been real. Just a result of the rhythm of the song that had played.

Fool. Idiot. They were only a few of the names he called himself. He took a deep breath. "Okay. I should go."

She started to reach out and touch his arm, but let her hand drop short of him. "You don't have to. We could watch a movie or something."

He shook his head. "Another time. I'll see you later, Ace."

Then he opened the apartment door and walked out. When the door shut behind him, it felt as if he'd left something behind that he would never get back.

And it made him want to hang his head and cry.

CHAPTER ELEVEN

THE DOOR TO the Border Patrol office felt heavy as Sherri opened it and stepped inside. She had flutters in her stomach that had little to do with returning to work after eight weeks and more to do with having to face Dez. What in the world had he been thinking, kissing her like that? What scared her more was how positively she'd responded. There had been no thoughts of friendship then. Instead, her heart had wanted more of Dez, while her brain reminded her that it could never happen.

What would she say when she saw him again? How would he act? Why did their dynamic have to change? She wanted to curse him for upsetting the status quo of their relationship, but he was Dez. He was her friend and partner. She trusted him still.

Right?

She went to her old desk, pulled her gun from her purse and placed the weapon in the drawer. There was no one at Dez's desk.

"Lopez, my office. Now."

She took a deep breath and then walked to her superior's office, taking a seat across from him. "I handed all my paperwork into HR so I could return."

"That's not why I called you in." He stood and grabbed a stack of files from the top of his desk and placed them on her lap. "Welcome to your new assignment. Background checks."

She groaned and flipped through the top dozen files. "Cap—"

"Desk duty like we discussed."

She'd hoped he'd forgotten about that. "But you need me in the field."

He paused and looked down at her. "I do. But I need you to be healthy more than I need you on the streets."

She shifted the files in her arms so they wouldn't slip and fall to the floor. "You're wasting my talents on this."

"Yep." He stood and walked back behind his desk. She flipped through a few more folders. He pointed to the door. "We're done here."

She stood, practically snapping to attention. "Thank you, sir." She hugged the folders to her chest and returned to her desk and let them fall, covering the top of it.

The office door opened, and Dez entered with Ras. The breath caught in her throat as Dez walked toward her, but he kept up his conversation with Ras and only gave a nod in her direction.

Ras laughed at something Dez said, then looked Sherri up and down. "So you're back."

She held out her hands to the folders littering her desk. "Assigned to background checks."

"Guess I'll have to find a new desk. I borrowed yours while you were out." Ras opened the lower desk drawer and pulled out a notepad and a half-eaten bag of chips. "Thanks for the loaner."

Dez held out his chair to Ras. "You can take mine. I'll move closer to the window."

And farther away from her. She tried not to take it personally, and forced a smile. "Good. It's settled, then."

She booted up her computer and logged in to the station with her badge number and password. It had expired and she had to change it. She chose "Dezsucks2!" and pressed Save. At least that brought a grin to her face.

For the first half of the day, she organized the files in terms of priority, then made a timetable as to when the checks needed to be completed. She stifled a yawn as she saved the spreadsheet on her computer. Her stomach growled and she realized she hadn't eaten since last night, beyond drinking a cup of coffee that morning. She looked up to find Dez watching her, but then he quickly started a discussion with Ras.

Would they ever be able to go back to the way things were?

She got her purse and stood. Ras looked up from what he'd been working on and glanced at his watch. "Going to lunch?"

"It's after twelve, so I figured I'd step out."

Ras glanced at Dez, then back at Sherri. "You want to join us? Maybe you can tell me war stories about being this guy's partner?"

She looked at Dez, but he didn't acknowledge the invitation. Sherri shook her head. "Maybe another time."

She left without looking back. Once outside the office, she leaned against the wall and fought back the tears that threatened. She wouldn't let him see he had hurt her.

RAS WAS TRYING to get his attention, but Dez kept his gaze on his computer monitor. "What was that all about?"

Dez sighed and looked up. "Need something?"

"An explanation. You and Sherri fighting or something?"

Or something described it perfectly. A coolness had formed between them and he feared that it would forever alter what they once had. "Doesn't matter. There's a lead that I want to track down before lunch. You coming?"

"Since I am your partner, yes."

Dez didn't wait for him, but pulled his suit coat from the back of his chair and walked out of the office. He strode down the hallway and to the bank of elevators. Sherri stood there, waiting. She looked up at him and froze. He turned left and took the stairs.

He waited in the lobby for Ras, who had taken the elevator down with Sherri. She wouldn't look at him, but breezed past him and out the front doors.

Ras shook his head.

His new partner didn't have to understand about his old one. There were no rules that stated he had to explain himself. Problem was, he didn't understand it himself.

He and Ras drove toward the Detroit River and the warehouse district. Dez pulled into the parking lot of the warehouse they'd raided not three months before. All these warehouses surrounding the riverfront, why had this been the one they had raided? Something didn't quite add up with the investigation.

He got out of the car and walked around, looking at the buildings that surrounded them. An import-export warehouse. A nightclub. An auto parts distributor. And finally, the warehouse that was supposed to hold an electronics manufacturer. Instead, it sheltered drugs smuggled into the country from Canada.

Ras asked, "What are we supposed to be seeing?"

"I don't know." Dez moved past his partner to the pier, where he gazed out across the river at the horizon. "What do you think is the distance between us and Windsor from here?"

"Maybe a mile? Maybe less."

Dez nodded and turned back to the warehouse. "Could you swim a mile across the river?"

"I could, but I wouldn't want to in that water. Would you?" Ras gave a shudder. "You're thinking they're bringing the drugs over by swimming them across?"

"Maybe."

"Okay, but what does that have to do with who squealed the details about the raid?"

"Nothing." Dez pulled out his cell phone and took several pictures. "But it could solve part of the mystery of how the drugs are getting here. Now we need to figure out who would profit more by betraying us."

"That's easy." When he gave Ras a look,

Ras continued, "Someone who didn't want any more interference. Kill some federal agents and they'll be investigating the shooting, rather than trying to find out how drugs are being transported."

Dez smiled. "Exactly." He rubbed his belly. "Ready for lunch?" He started to walk away.

Ras called after him, "I don't understand you."

"My old partner doesn't, either, so you're not alone." He slid into the car, ready to think of something else besides this case.

SHERRI PUSHED HER uneaten dinner away. Mama frowned at her. "Are you feeling sick?"

"I'm not hungry." She needed something besides food, but she wasn't sure what that was. "I know you went to all that trouble to make it."

Mama stood and took her plate to the kitchen counter and scraped her dinner into a plastic container and searched for its lid. "I'll pack it up for you to take home when you're ready."

Her dad cleared his throat, and she

turned to face him. “Something bothering you, *mija*?” he asked.

The list for that grew longer by the day. Instead, she shook her head. “Just tired. Maybe I wasn’t ready to go back to work.”

He reached out and took her hand. “You’ll get stronger. You must be patient.”

“Yes, but then I have another chemo appointment and the cycle starts all over again.” She shook her head. “Sorry. It’s been kinda rough lately.”

“Dez must be glad you’re back at work.”

Sherri gave a half-hearted chuckle. “Actually, it’s the opposite. We’re not talking right now.”

Mama came directly over to her at the kitchen table. “But I saw the two of you on the dance floor last Saturday night. You two looked so close. What happened?”

“He told me he loved me.” With those few words, he had changed their friendship and now she was afraid they’d never recover what they’d had.

Mama clapped her hands. “It’s about time that man shared his feelings with you.”

“And I told him we had to stay friends.”

"What? Why did you say that, *mija*?" Mama groaned and buried her head in her hands. "I've never seen any man love you the way he does. So completely. Never wavering. Even with all you've been through these past months, he never left your side. Always there."

She knew everything he had done for her, so why did he have to mess things up between them? She wished he'd never kissed her. Never told her. She'd rather be clueless and go on as they had before. She couldn't do that anymore. "And I don't want that to change."

"Why would loving him back change what you have?"

"Because it would. It has to." Sherri wiped at the tear that formed in the corner of her eye. "All I need is my friend right now. But he changed it, and I don't know if we can get it back."

"Of course you can." Mama leaned over and took Sherri's hand. "That is, if you want to get it back."

She wanted her old friend and partner

like before. “I do, but he won’t even look at me.”

“Then call him.”

She burst out laughing as if that was the funniest suggestion that she had ever heard. “And say what, Mama? Don’t give up on me? Let’s be friends? Would it really be that simple?”

“Why not? You two could always say anything to each other. Why should it be different now?”

Sherri doubted her mother, but Mama had never been wrong before. Could it be so easy?

SHERRI WAITED FOR Ras to go home for the night before approaching Dez at his desk. She put her hands on the armrests of his chair, trapping him and forcing him to look at her. “You need to stop shutting me out. Talk to me.”

Anger blazed in his eyes. Good. It was better than indifference. “What is there to talk about? You made yourself very clear about what you want from me.”

“Yes, your friendship. But you’re acting

as if I've betrayed you somehow." She let go of the chair and sat on the corner of his desk. It was now or never. "Dez, I was honest with you."

"No, I was the one who was honest with you." He stood so that she had to look up into his face. "You're running away from the feelings you have for me. And for what? To hold on to a job? Or to keep me at a distance because pursuing something more than friendship scares you more than dealing with cancer?"

Was he serious? He didn't know what he was talking about. "You have no clue what I'm dealing with, so don't stand there and tell me what I think and what I feel."

He put his finger in her face. "I know better than anyone else. I'm the one you share things with. The one who is there for you, but what do I get in return?"

"So because you do nice things, I'm supposed to, what? Date you?" She shook her head. "Do you hear what you're saying?"

"What I don't hear is that you have the same feelings for me, but you punish me for expressing mine."

The captain's office door swung open, and the man stood in the doorway. "Lopez! Jackson! Get in here now."

Sherri glared at Dez before breezing past him into the captain's office. She closed her eyes and took a few deep breaths.

Dez came to stand next to her while Captain White slammed the door shut and walked behind his desk. "Whatever is going on between the two of you stops *now.*"

Dez cleared his throat. He spoke quietly as he said, "There's nothing going on, sir. Just a disagreement."

The captain pounced at Dez's words. "A disagreement that is affecting my other agents and the atmosphere in this office. The tension between you two is so thick, we can all see it when you're both in the same room."

Sherri glanced at Dez. "We'll resolve it, sir."

"See that you do, or I'm transferring one of you out of this office. I won't put up with two agents who can't get along." Captain White sat down behind his desk.

"What happened? You two were my best agents who always had each other's back." He peered at Sherri. "Is it the desk duty assignment? You know that's temporary."

She nodded. "I do. But no, sir, it's a personal disagreement."

"Well, keep the personal out of this office." He pointed at the both of them. "Do you hear me? I won't hesitate to make changes for what's best for this organization. Though frankly I'd hate to lose either one of you. Now go!"

"Yes, sir." Dez opened the door and motioned for Sherri to walk past him. She motioned for him to go first instead. He scowled. As he went toward his desk, she heard him muttering, "I will not be transferred from here."

"I won't, either," she said, kicking her voice up a notch. "So we have to get along." It was still hard to look at him, her best friend and partner. They used to be so close, to have the same mind about things. But now they couldn't be in the same space as each other, much less talk civilly.

She went to her desk and got her things.

"Dez, I'll see you tomorrow. Maybe a night's sleep will give us both perspective."

He gave a curt nod, but said nothing.

DEZ WATCHED SHERRI leave and collapsed into his chair. She was right. They both needed to get some perspective on their relationship. If there was one they could save.

He closed his eyes. How had they gotten to this place? He loved her. Truly loved her. He wanted only the best for her and yet now he couldn't look at her without the hurt rising in his chest. Hurt that she wouldn't give them a chance. Angry that it had taken this long to act on his feelings, and now he could lose her anyway.

Captain White's office door opened. He scanned the room, only a few agents were still there, then his eyes fell on Dez. "Agent Lopez leave?" he asked.

"Yes, sir."

"Do you want to talk about it?"

Dez was confused. The captain didn't talk about feelings. Ever. He shook his head. "No offense, sir, but this is something I need to work out on my own."

The captain nodded and he turned, his

phone had begun to ring. Dez could hear it from where he was.

The captain preoccupied, Dez logged off his computer and left the office. The temperature had risen enough that his shirt stuck to his back by the time he'd gotten to his car. Inside, he turned the air-conditioning up full blast. As Dez drove home, he promised himself he'd add central air to the house once he could save enough money. For now, he'd strip down to a pair of shorts and switch on all the fans.

After dinner he settled in front of the television with a cold beer but couldn't focus on the ball game. Instead, Sherri came to mind as she always did these days. They needed to work together. But for that to happen, he needed to let go of his feelings for her.

Maybe he was wrong. Maybe she didn't love him, at least not the way he wanted her to. Could he let go of his hopes and stay friends? The role of friend had started to chafe though. He wanted more. Needed more. Yet, if he pushed, he'd lose her. And that was worse than her not sharing his feelings. He needed her in his life, even if it was in a supporting role and not as his girlfriend.

He took a pull on the bottle, let the liquid slide down his throat. Put the bottle to his forehead so that the condensation would cool him.

That was what he would do with Sherri. He would let things cool until he could handle the heat of his love for her so that neither one of them would get burned.

In the middle of the night, his cell phone rang from the nightstand. Dez groaned and reached across the bed to answer the call. The caller ID said Sherri. He paused. But what if something was wrong? “Sherri, are you okay?”

“I wasn’t sure if you’d answer.”

“Sure I would. Just tell me you’re okay.”

Silence. “I can’t sleep. I’ve been thinking.”

He tensed, not wanting to have this conversation. He’d been avoiding her at work for that very reason until it had boiled over earlier that day. He didn’t need to hear again how they should stay friends. But he couldn't say that, so he asked, "What's bothering you?"

"The warehouse."

Okay. He hadn't expected that. He sat up and turned on the light by his bed. "What about the warehouse?"

"We checked into the backgrounds of the owners of the building because we figured it'd take money to run this kind of operation, but what about the workers they employed? We never checked their backgrounds, right? What if the drug runners are connected to the employees?"

It seemed obvious to him now. "So we looked in the wrong direction."

"Right. An employee could be using the spot on the weekends when the owners are away or gone to do other business."

"And they bring the drugs in at night or during off-hours when no one in management is there."

"Yes."

He liked where she was going with this. He'd have to jump on the lead in the morning when he got to the office. "So that's what kept you awake?"

She hesitated again and he feared what

she might say next. “I have another chemo coming up, I’ve been worrying about it. I don’t like how it makes me feel.”

“Number five out of six or so. You’ve almost finished and then we can celebrate.”

“Can we?”

He swallowed. “Absolutely we can. If you can forgive me for acting like an idiot.”

A low chuckle sounded through the phone. “But it comes to you so naturally,” she joked.

He could almost picture her smiling. “Thanks for that.”

“You deserve it.”

“And more.”

Silence on both sides. Then Dez looked at his alarm clock. “It’s almost three thirty. Want to meet for breakfast? Then we can go over your ideas. Maybe come up with a plan before we get into the office.”

“Sure. Give me about fifteen minutes to change and I’ll meet you at Lolly’s. If you get there first, get me an iced tea.”

“Tea?”

“I can’t drink coffee lately. My tolerance of what I can eat and drink has changed.”

“All right, iced tea it is.” He wondered

how much he should say while their truce remained fragile. "Thank you for calling me."

"There's no one else in my life that's like you, Dez."

DEZ HAD ALREADY arrived at the greasy spoon by the time she walked through the door of Lolly's. Sherri bypassed the other diners and sat down in the booth where he waited. He asked, "Did you get any sleep?"

She shrugged and put her purse on the seat next to her. "I'll be fine. Everyone already expects me to walk around with dark circles under my eyes. What's a few shades darker?"

"You need your rest."

She picked up the menu and pretended to be engrossed in it even though she already knew what she was ordering. If she was honest, she already knew what Dez would order, too. They rarely strayed from their favorites.

She put the menu down, unwrapped a straw and placed it in her iced tea, and took a sip. She glanced around the diner. "Quite a crowd for predawn."

"I mean it, Sherri. You have to take care of yourself."

She frowned at him. "I know that. But when I can't sleep, what am I supposed to do?"

"Have you told your doctor about the insomnia?"

She almost sighed in relief as a waitress arrived to take their orders. After the server left, Sherri played with the straw wrapper, winding it between her fingers. "She'd only prescribe another medication. I'm on five or six already. I keep losing count. I don't want to take any more than I have to."

"But if you're not sleeping—"

"It's fine. Drop it."

He opened his mouth to say something but changed his mind. They sipped their drinks and watched each other. Finally, Sherri reached her hand across the table and took Dez's in hers. "Are we going to talk about it now?"

He removed his hand from hers. "Do we need to?"

Yes. Because if they didn't, they'd lose each other. Perhaps for good. "You haven't really spoken to me since I returned to work. What's up with that?"

"It goes both ways, you know."

She folded her hands together and placed them on the table in front of her. "I do know, which is why I've tried to start conversations with you, but it's like you shut down. You couldn't even look at me."

He looked away. "Maybe because I was ashamed of how I acted."

She shook her head. "Why? You were a perfect gentleman that night."

"Who pressed his advantage when you weren't ready."

She offered a small smile. "It was just one kiss."

But that kiss had caused more harm than good. She understood where he was coming from, but if they put too much importance on it, then they wouldn't be able to get back to the friendship they'd once enjoyed.

Dez set his coffee cup down and motioned to the waitress for a refill. He finally looked at Sherri. "It meant more than a kiss and you know it. But I'll take your lead. I'll push down these feelings and we can stay friends."

She let out a breath and nodded in relief. "It's what's best for us right now."

He watched her intently before saying, "We'll have to agree to disagree on that."

CHAPTER TWELVE

DEZ WENT TO pick Luke up from the kid's apartment. His mother watched Dez with a sour expression on her face, as if he were taking her baby boy away from her. Which maybe he was. Luke came into the kitchen and put the paper bag he carried on the floor beside his feet. "Well, Mom, this is it."

She wiped at her eyes, then pulled her son into her arms. "You write me every day. Hear? Every. Day."

Luke hugged her tightly. "Promise." He let go of her and leaned down for his bag. He looked over at Dez. "We should go. Don't want to be late."

At the front door, Luke turned around one last time. "I'll be okay, Mom. And I'll send you whatever money I can."

His mom nodded. "Just come back."

Luke stepped into the hallway and Dez

gave a nod to Donna, then followed the boy toward the stairs. Boy about to become a man, heading off to boot camp.

Soon they were at the car. Luke clutched his paper bag as he sat in the passenger seat, not saying a word. Dez drove to the bus station, trying to think of more advice to share. But he found none. They sat in silence, both lost in their thoughts.

For Dez, this brought up memories of his own journey to joining the Marine Corps. He remembered the anticipation and the fear. He glanced at Luke, who was focused straight ahead. Dez slugged Luke's shoulder. The kid smiled at him. "Knock it off. You won't be able to do that much longer, old man."

"I know." Dez knocked Luke's shoulder again. "So I've got to get all my shots in now."

The ride didn't take long. They arrived at the bus station and Dez parked the car. He turned to Luke. "You got your ticket?"

Luke nodded as he stared at the bus station. "They sent it last week." He faced Dez. "I'm making the right decision?"

Dez raised one eyebrow at this. "That a question?"

Luke shook his head. "No. I did choose right. I know it." He opened the car door and stepped out. Dez got out, too, and walked around the car to stand next to Luke.

"Do you want me to go up there with you?" Dez offered.

Luke took a while to answer him. "Nah. I've got to do this myself." He held out his hand to Dez. "Thank you for everything."

Dez glanced at the hand, then pulled the kid into a rib-crushing hug. "You take care of yourself, okay? You have my address and number just in case."

Luke nodded and Dez pulled out his wallet and took a few twenties out and thrust them into the kid's hand. "For snacks on the bus and once you get on base."

"Thanks, Dez. Besides my mom and sister, you're the closest thing I have to family."

"I know, kid. I feel the same way. I've got you and Sherri." He tried to smile. "That's a pretty good family in my book."

Luke held up the money clutched in his hand. "I owe you."

"And I plan on collecting, so you keep out of trouble." He leaned back against the car. "Don't forget to call your mom tonight when you get there."

"I will." The kid looked like he was going to say something else, but then he started to head for the bus station doors, holding one hand up in farewell.

Dez watched him until he entered the building, then wiped at the moisture in the corners of his eyes before getting back in his car and heading home.

SHERRI FINISHED THE background check she'd been working on and saved the results on her computer. The crick in her neck had started to annoy her, so she stood up.

In mid-stretch, she tried to figure out what she was feeling. She didn't have any pain. No nausea. She felt a little tired, sure, but fatigue had become her constant companion. So what was this?

She felt…normal. A different normal than she had felt before cancer, but still. Normal. She smiled then covered that with her hand. April had promised that she would get to this point one day, but she'd thought it would be much later. After chemo and radiation. After reconstruction surgery. After all of it. And yet here she was, finding her new normal.

Dez and Ras entered the office and approached her. "We need some advice, Ace." Dez passed her some notes, which he'd obviously written since most of it was illegible. He pointed to a name that he'd circled. "We've got a list of employees from that company that operates out of the warehouse. We've still got a few people we're checking on, but this guy we're having a hard time finding out about, which seems suspicious. Harold Weston. Does that name sound familiar?"

She shook her head. Dez pulled over a chair so that he could sit next to her as they reviewed his notes. She could smell the aftershave he'd put on that morning. He drummed his fingers on her desk. "I'm still confused as to why we have so little intel on this Weston. It just doesn't follow. Apart from the bare details, there's nothing. I'm betting there could be a connection between Weston and the drug cartel?"

She kept looking through his notes, then asked, "Does the connection have to be Weston himself with the cartel? Maybe it's someone related to Weston who has the in with the drug runners?" She handed back the pages.

Dez waggled his finger at her. "You might be onto something there."

Ras jotted something down and walked to his computer. He typed some information in and scrolled through a few screens. "Two brothers and a sister."

"All right. We'll start there." Dez nodded at Sherri. "Thanks, Ace."

"You bet. That's what I'm here for."

DEZ CHECKED HIS mailbox when he got home and noticed that a letter from Luke had arrived. He smiled as he ripped it open and took it inside to read. The kid hated boot camp, but he understood why the drill sergeants used the tactics they did. The kid was too smart for his own good.

His cell phone buzzed and he glanced at

the screen. "Hey, Mateo. You coming to the game tomorrow night?"

"If I can get away. Listen. Do you have plans tonight? I was hoping you could help me with something."

"What's going on?"

"His name is Marcus and he needs a mentor maybe even more than Luke did." It sounded like Mateo had covered the phone, a muffled conversation was happening without Dez being able to make out the words. Then Mateo was back. "I'm downtown right now at the juvenile courts, hoping to get him out on bail before they finish for the night."

Dez checked the time. "It's after five already."

"I know. A hearing ran late, but I might be able to get in front of the judge before he goes home. He owes me."

Dez wasn't sure if he wanted to get involved again with another kid. Sure, he'd gotten lucky with Luke, but not every kid was like him. "I don't know what I'll be able to do."

"Having you stand with us could help his case. He's not a bad kid."

Dez smirked at that. "To you, they never are."

"He's stuck in a rough situation and I want to give him a chance to get out of it. He's from Mack and Concord."

Dez closed his eyes, knowing he'd already agreed to help before Mateo had even mentioned his old neighborhood. He'd been that kid himself once. "I'm leaving now. Which court?"

Mateo gave him the directions and Dez drove there as quickly as he could. He hadn't changed his clothes yet, so he was still dressed in suit and tie, appropriate for court. He parked in the municipal parking lot then jogged up to the courthouse. Mateo waved him over when Dez cleared the metal detectors. A kid no older than eleven sat on a bench, staring at the floor. "What did he do?"

"Flashed a gun in a park where kids were playing." Mateo shook his head. "He was supposed to shoot someone as part of a gang initiation. But someone called in the incident and Marcus chickened out."

Eleven was too young to be worrying about getting into a gang. Heck, eleven was to young to be worrying about anything. "Whose gun?"

"Unregistered." Mateo closed his eyes. "And the police officer who responded to the call is convinced he wasn't going to discharge it, which means Marcus is only being held on illegal possession of a firearm, although that is bad enough." He gave a big sigh. "The cop knows the kid and the foster family, so he gave me a call."

Dez looked over at Marcus. "What does he say?"

"Hasn't said a word."

Dez nodded, then held up a finger. "Let me talk to him." He walked down the short hallway and sat on the bench next to Marcus. The kid didn't even look at him. "You from Mack Avenue, too? I grew up on Helen." The kid didn't answer him. "Tough neighborhood. Lots of gangs." The kid stirred, but still didn't look at him or say anything.

The judge's chamber door opened and Mateo sprinted over. He stopped to glance at Dez, Dez nodded and Mateo closed the chamber door behind him.

"Mr. Lopez is a good man, Marcus. A

good lawyer. He's trying to help you out." He paused. "But you've got to give him something."

Marcus snapped up his head to glare at Dez. "I'm no snitch."

"He's not asking you to rat out the guys who put you up to this, but you need to tell your side of the story to the judge." Marcus didn't say anything else and Dez doubted he could help this kid if he didn't want to help himself. "Mr. Lopez will be coming out soon to get you in front of the judge. We expect you to show respect and answer his questions truthfully."

Marcus's eyes looked too old and wary as he stared at Dez, as if he'd seen too much at such a young age. *"We?"*

"Us foster kids from Mack Ave. have to stick up for each other, right? I'll go in there with you if you want."

The kid's expression knocked him back. Dez could remember that same skepticism and disillusionment being on his own face at that age. Marcus scowled and returned his gaze to the floor. The chamber door opened and Mateo motioned for them to join him inside. Dez put his hand on the kid's shoulder. "This is it, Marcus. Good luck in there."

The kid stood and took a few steps before turning back to face Dez. "Aren't you coming with me?"

APRIL CALLED SHERRI and again invited her to the Hope Center for a support group meeting. "It's been a benefit to me, especially since I don't have any family in the area. I couldn't have gone through what I did alone."

Sherri wasn't convinced. The idea of talking about what was happening to her in front of a group of strangers didn't exactly sound like a good time. "What do they do again?"

"Most people discuss the effects of the cancer. Treatments. Even their hopes and fears."

Still didn't sound like something Sherri would volunteer to be a part of. However, two nights later Sherri arrived at the address that Page had told her to write down. So, this was it.

The Hope Center took up one of the storefronts in a strip mall on the north end of Detroit near Eight Mile. It looked out of place next to the cell phone and liquor stores. She parked, then got out of her car, hitting the fob to make sure the doors were locked. She walked up to the center and peered in the window. April saw her and waved. She walked over and motioned her inside.

When Sherri entered, April approached her and gave her a hug. "I wasn't sure if you'd make it."

"I said I would. And I keep my promises even when I'm not sure about something like this."

April escorted her over to the coordinator, who handed her a sticker for a name tag. Sherri raised one eyebrow at this.

Page rolled her eyes. "They like to be able to call us by our names, but they've seen me enough around here they don't need me to wear a name tag anymore."

Sherri wrote her name on the sticker, then removed the backing and stuck the tag to her chest. "It could be worse."

Page leaned in to whisper to her. "Never say those words here. You can always find worse."

Page took a seat in one of the metal folding chairs. Sherri sat next to her and April brought them each a glass of lemonade. Page told April no, thanks, but Sherri accepted her cup and took a sip. It was overly sweet. She tried not to make a face.

The coordinator introduced herself, then had everyone go around the room saying his or her name and stage of cancer. When it came to Sherri's turn, she kept her eyes on her hands that she'd folded in her lap. "I'm Sherri. Stage two."

Page was next. "You know I'm Page. Breast cancer twice. And now my husband has served me with divorce papers. So... yay me."

"Chad did what?" April gaped at her. "Why didn't you say anything?"

Page gave a one-shoulder shrug. "I just did."

"I thought we were friends. You couldn't tell me before this?" April turned back to the group. "I'm April. Stage three and I'm about to have my reconstruction surgery." She glowered at Page. "And can I say that I'm not happy that my so-called best friend has been keeping things from me?"

Page wouldn't look at April. Sherri couldn't help but notice. "I didn't want to bring you down, April. You're doing so well."

"But I could help you through this."

Page grimaced at April, her eyes sad. "How? He wants out of our marriage and can I blame him? I haven't exactly been a load of laughs lately. What can you do to help? You can't change it." Page folded her arms over her chest and turned to the coordinator. "Lynn, tell her that she's overreacting."

The coordinator colored slightly and fidgeted in her chair. "Page, we've talked about how we are all entitled to our own feelings. If April feels angry, then you have to accept that."

"Then she has to accept that I didn't want to burden her with my divorce."

April opened her mouth to say something, but the coordinator cut them both off by having them stand in the center of the circle. They stood back-to-back. "Now each of you give one word about what you need from the other. April?"

"Honesty."

Page started to turn, but Lynn forced her to remain with her back to April. "I didn't lie about anything."

Lynn held up one finger. "She is letting you know what she needs from you. Hear it. Accept it."

Page put her hands on her hips. "I'll accept it and I'll be honest. Even when doing so could hurt her or make her sad."

Lynn gave a nod and kept her gaze on Page. "And what do you need from April?"

Page shook her head. "This is ridiculous."

"Just let her know what you need from her," Lynn repeated.

Page leaned back against April. "Space. Is that honest enough?"

A murmur among the other participants rose and fell as the two women in the center turned and looked at each other. April put her arms around Page. "Thank you."

"I just told you that I need you to back off." But Page accepted the hug. At least until she pushed April away from her.

"But you're being honest with me instead of going along with what I want. That's what I need from you."

"Well, you can be a lot to take sometimes with all your positive thinking and Miss Merry Sunshine attitude."

April smiled widely. "Yes, I can."

Page peered at her. "There are times when I need to be alone."

"I can accept that."

"And you're not upset?"

"I'm more upset when you don't communicate with me about what you're really feeling." She put an arm around Page's shoulders. "Can you accept that?"

Page nodded and the two women hugged again.

Sherri watched all this with surprise. So honest and open in front of all these people. She wasn't going to have to do the same kind of thing on her first visit, was she? She clutched the pamphlet she'd been given and fanned herself with it, more to have something to do than watching the display of emotion in the center of the circle. This was definitely out of her wheelhouse.

Lynn turned to the rest of the group. "Who would like to continue our sharing time?"

Luckily, someone else talked about how

they were having doubts about how best to handle sharing the news of her cancer. Sherri settled back into her chair.

Page, who had returned to her seat, whispered, "They won't make you say anything tonight, but April will tell you that it helps to share."

April encouraged from her seat, "It really does."

Sherri smirked at her. These two couldn't be any more different, yet she appreciated them both being a part of her journey.

After the meeting the three women stood next to April's car. "What did you think of tonight? And be honest," April asked.

Sherri shrugged. "This isn't really my thing. At least I didn't think so before I came. But I feel better about myself so maybe that's good. I don't feel so isolated. There're others like me out there struggling with the same issues. And, in a weird way, that's a comfort."

April nodded and grinned. "I'm glad, too. Maybe we'll see you at next month's meeting." She unlocked her car door with her fob. "So my surgery is going to be next month and I'd love it if you could both be there. Because someday, it will be your turn to be at the end of this and have a new body, too."

Page looked down at her flat chest. "I don't know if I'm going the reconstruction route. I've never had much to start with, and right now my goal is to just get through this."

"You could change your mind when you see how fabulous I'm going to look." April struck a pose, which made Page scoff, but Sherri noticed the smile playing around her mouth.

"You seem so upbeat after all this, April. Why aren't you angry like the rest of us?" Sherri asked her.

April adjusted the strap of her purse higher onto her shoulder. "I could be bitter, but what's that going to do? Mostly I feel lucky. I've stared death in the face and made him blink. I'm ready to celebrate my new life with a new body and attitude." She pulled out her journal. "While I was sick, I wrote down everything I wanted to do once I was healthy again. And I'm going to start working on each thing and cross them off one by one."

Sherri was eager to see what the journal contained. "What kinds of things are on that list?"

Page rolled her eyes. "Oh, don't get her started."

April opened the journal and pointed to a line. "Go see a musical on Broadway." She smiled, then hugged the book to her chest. "I've always wanted to go and now I will."

Sherri didn't want to admit that she was jealous of April's optimistic outlook. "I haven't even thought about what it will be like when my treatment is over. I'm still trying to make it to tomorrow."

April turned a page and then another. "So just name one thing you would want once you're healthy again. Where do you see your life after cancer?"

An image of Dez filled her brain and she gasped. Page's eyes widened at this. "Wow, it must be good. What did you see?"

"Not what. Who." Sherri's hands shook as she fumbled for her keys inside her purse. "I have to go."

"You running away from this?" Page asked.

No. This time she wasn't running away.

In fact, maybe she should try moving toward it. But she couldn't have Dez. They'd finally gotten back on track with their friendship, so why would her brain even be thinking about this? She blamed it on all the sharing that had happened in the support group. "I'll talk to you guys later. Thanks for inviting me."

"You don't have to be scared about what you want," April said.

"I'm not scared." But her heart fluttered and her body shuddered from the thought of Dez. "Good night."

"I've got to get to work, anyway. Yay, night shift." Page waved to them both and walked to her car.

April squeezed Sherri's hand. "I hope you get what you want."

They said their goodbyes again and Sherri got into her car, but didn't put the key in the ignition. Instead, she sat in the parking lot while she contemplated where to go. She should go home, but the idea of being alone in her apartment didn't appeal.

Eventually, she pulled out of the parking lot and drove aimlessly, debating whether she should stop at her parents' place to see how they were. Strangely, she found herself looking up at Dez's house. How had she gotten here? She remembered making the turns to arrive at this destination, but couldn't recall why.

She stared at the closed front door for ten minutes until finally she switched off the ignition. She took a deep breath, then opened the car door and stepped outside. She watched for signs of Dez. Maybe he wasn't home? Maybe he had gone out?

Or maybe he had opened the front door and stepped out on the porch to watch her.

She could wave, get back in her car and leave. Tell him later she'd forgotten why she stopped by. But something about April's list made her walk around the car and up the sidewalk to Dez. He waited on the top step, not moving. She stood on the bottom step and looked up at him.

"Did we have plans tonight?"

She shook her head.

"Are you okay?"

Another shake of her head.

"Sherri, what is it? What's wrong?"

She opened her mouth, but couldn't say a word. Didn't know what to say. Couldn't understand the swirl of emotions that had brought her there. She closed her eyes.

She shouldn't be there.

She started to leave, but Dez bolted down the steps and began to follow her. He put a hand on her shoulder to stop her. He turned her around, about to say something, when his cell phone buzzed. He sighed and slipped the phone from his back pocket. "It's Ras. Give me a moment, then we can talk about this." He answered the call. She watched him while he talked. He glanced at her and swore loud enough for her to hear, then hung up.

"Problems?"

"I have to go. Ras thinks he's found the mole."

Sherri took a step toward her car. "I'm going with you."

"No, you're not." When she opened her mouth to protest, he numbered the reasons using his fingers. "You're assigned to desk duty. You're not armed. You're not a hundred percent healthy, which could compromise your judgment and your reaction times."

"I'm fine and you know it. You need me to back the two of you up."

He raised one eyebrow at this. "With what gun?"

"Your Magnum that you have locked in your safe." She knew the code to get in if he wouldn't get it for her, but she'd give him the chance to help her.

He shook his head. "I can't."

"Why not? We used to go into these situations every day, so what's changed? And so help me if you say cancer."

His eyes focused on hers, heat filling them. "I can't focus on the situation if I'm worried about you and your safety."

That heat in his eyes made her brow damp and she reached up to wipe away the moisture. "I'll be fine. I'm trained for situations like this. Same as you."

"All right. But if the cap comes down on me, I'm pointing the finger at you." He left her and returned shortly with the Magnum. He handed it to her and locked his house before going over to her car. "You drive. I'll call Ras and tell him we're on our way."

Dez barked out directions as Sherri drove them to a pier on the Detroit River that was less than a half mile from the Canadian shore. They parked near a blue sedan that belonged to Ras, but he was nowhere to be found. Sherri started to get out of the car when Dez reached over and grabbed her hand. She turned back to him and he pulled her into a quick kiss. "Just in case."

She found it impossible to squelch her smile. "And you say I'm the pessimistic one."

Quietly, they stole along the edge of a building that bordered the pier. Dez stopped and she followed suit. "What is it? What do you see?"

He answered without turning to face her, his focus on the pier. "She's got a gun on Ras."

Sherri peered around him and saw a woman holding a gun on Ras. "She's the mole?"

Dez whispered, "Her lover is…or was a guy named Jones. He was killed earlier this month, but she was married to a DEA agent who died in the raid. We've been watching her this last week, since we discovered her connection to both sides of the case. Tonight she was planning to disappear."

He'd obviously been busy lately. "How did you figure that out?"

He turned to her and smiled. "It's my job." He turned back to watch the interaction between Ras and the woman. He tucked his gun into the back of his jeans. "I've got to go out there before she does something stupid like shoot my partner. You stay here and back me up."

Fat chance. Like she'd let him go out there without her? "I won't stand here and do nothing, Dez."

"Then keep an eye out for anyone else who wants to join our party." He stepped back and kissed her real quick again. "We need to talk later."

Then he left her and strode out onto the pier, his hands raised.

"MIRANDA."

She pulled Ras against her and held the gun to his temple. "Not nice, Ras," she said. "You didn't tell me you were bringing your partner tonight."

Ras grunted as she tightened her grip on his throat. "Didn't get a chance," he rasped.

"Don't do anything stupid." Dez walked

slowly toward them, not wanting to make her skittish enough to pull the trigger. "We only want to talk. You don't have to hang on to this guilt, Miranda. You didn't know your husband would die."

The woman chuckled. "Didn't I? I only wanted to warn Omarian. I didn't think he'd kill Steve in the process. All that blood is on my hands."

Dez noticed that she clenched the gun with force, and he tensed, ready to shoot if necessary.

"After…he got scared and was going to confess. I couldn't let him do that. He would have ruined everything I've worked so hard to get."

Things clicked into place. "You're the one who shot him that day on the pier."

"I won't go to jail. I'll kill you and Ras before that happens." She pointed the gun at Dez, her finger twitching on the trigger.

Ras elbowed her in the side as Dez pulled his gun from behind him and got a shot off, hitting her in the shoulder. Something bit into his side, but he rushed forward, Sherri close behind him.

Ras had Miranda facedown on the pier

while she screamed and cursed at them. He struggled with getting the handcuffs on her. He glanced up at Dez. "Looks like you got hit."

Dez was confused at first, but then gingerly touched the red stain that had spread across his side.

Sherri shouted his name as he crumpled onto the pier. She ran to him and knelt down to be close to him. "No."

He looked up at her. "This scene seems familiar, doesn't it?"

"We don't have to take turns getting shot, you know."

She ripped off the corner of her shirt and shoved it into his wound. He hissed at the pressure and pain that traveled up his side. "Gently. Please."

She pressed harder. "I've got to stop the blood."

He could barely hear Ras on his cell phone calling the incident in because of the buzz that had started to fill his ears. He knew he only had moments left before he lost consciousness. He reached up and touched Sherri's face. "I do love you. Always."

She smiled as tears slid down her cheeks and mixed with the blood left there from his fingers. "I love you, too, so don't you dare die on me. I don't want a new partner or best friend."

"Promise."

APRIL MET THE ambulance outside the Emergency Room and groaned as Sherri jumped out and yelled orders to the paramedic. "Didn't we already do this with you?"

Sherri winced. "It's Dez's turn."

April checked Dez's wound and listened as the paramedic reviewed her notes and they sped down the hall to a trauma room. April pointed to Sherri. "You need to go to the waiting room."

Sherri shook her head. "I'm staying."

"I need to examine him and determine the damage."

Dez opened one eye and peered at April. "She's staying."

April raised one eyebrow and looked at Dez. "All right, Agent Hottie. She stays, but she hugs the wall or I have security escort her out of here."

Sherri nodded and kept to the wall as

April removed the gauze the paramedic had packed into Dez's wound.

"Can you take a deep breath for me?" April asked Dez.

Dez tried, but groaned and coughed. "It hurts."

"Appears the bullet broke a rib or two, but you're breathing clearly so it missed your lung." She probed his side with her fingers. "No exit wound so we'll have to do surgery to remove it." She pointed to a nurse. "Call upstairs and see who's available. I don't want to risk infection, he's going up to surgery now." She peered down at Dez. "Is there anyone we need to call?"

He looked over at Sherri. "The only one I'll ever need is here." He held out his hand to her, and she approached slowly and took it in hers. "You'll be here when I get out?"

"Always." She kissed his hand and April left the room for a moment. "I can't bear the thought of living without you, so you fight this and you come back to me."

He reached up and touched her lips with his finger. "I thought that was my line."

April reentered the trauma room. "They're

going to take him up now. I'll make sure you get updates, Sherri, but it could be an hour or so."

Sherri bent down and kissed him softly. "Why did it take two brushes with death for us to realize that we want a life together?"

"Maybe because we're too hardheaded and stubborn to realize it any other way."

As April pushed the gurney out the door, Sherri clung to Dez's hand until she had to let go. She stood and watched him as he disappeared down the hall and through the double doors toward surgery.

SHERRI PACED THE surgical waiting room and watched the clock. A little after midnight, her parents showed up. Mama opened her arms, and Sherri ran into them. "They took him in over an hour ago, and I haven't heard anything since."

Mama rubbed her back. "I'm glad you called us. Dez is family."

Sherri hung on to her mother tightly. "He is, Mama. And now that I realize how I feel about him, am I going to lose him already? We haven't had a chance to be together." She let go of Mama and glanced up, thinking she'd heard a doctor come in to give them news. But the doorway remained empty.

"Together as in friends?" Mama asked.

Sherri offered a wobbly smile. "Together as in a couple. You knew what I meant."

Mama gave her a warm smile. "Needed to hear the words out loud, *mija*, to be sure that you had really come to understand what that man means to you."

"Everything, Mama. He means everything." She wiped her eyes. "I can't imagine another day of my life without him."

Mama held Sherri's face in her hands. "I felt the same about your father. And that feeling never goes away."

April entered the waiting room, and Sherri rushed to hear the update on Dez. "Is he going to be okay?"

April told them, "The last I heard they've removed the bullet, but they're still trying to get the bleeding under control."

What if he lost too much blood? What if he died while they tried to save him? She couldn't accept that. Wouldn't let that thought enter her mind. She shook her head. "You didn't answer my question."

"Because I don't know that answer." April put a comforting hand on Sherri's arm. "You need to stay strong and keep believing in him. I'll be back if there are any more updates."

"Thanks, April."

Sherri turned back to Mama and burst into tears. Mama held her as she buried her face in her shoulder.

SHERRI OPENED HER eyes to find a white hospital pillow beneath her cheek and that she was resting on the bed beside Dez. She raised her head to find him watching her. "You're awake."

He smiled and placed a hand on hers. "So are you. Your snores woke me up."

"I told you I don't snore."

"Right." He shifted his weight and groaned at the pain in his side. "Am I going to make it?"

She'd waited impatiently for two hours, annoying everyone with her questions, she was so scared. Her parents such a blessing until he was out of surgery and in recovery.

April had assured her that the best surgeon had been called to operate on him.

But still, she hadn't been able to rest until she'd seen him lying unconscious but alive on the hospital bed. "Two broken ribs, and the bullet lodged into some muscle in your back. You're going to be sore for a while." She smirked at him. "And on desk duty with me."

He grinned at her. "As long as I'm with you, the rest of it doesn't matter."

She composed her face, and her tongue darted out to wet her lips. "Dez, I…"

He shook his head. "You love me, Sherri. I know you do. Don't even try to deny it."

"I wasn't going to deny anything, but we have a lot to think about." She squeezed his hand still holding hers. "This changes everything. What if…"

"What if I got shot? What if you got cancer? What if we got separated as partners at work? These are all things that we can figure out." He brought her hand to his lips and kissed it. "Our relationship is founded on our friendship, which means we'll be able to weather whatever life throws at us. Cancer. Bullets. Whatever. We'll be able to survive it because we're together. And I want to marry you as soon as I get out of this hospital."

She hadn't expected a proposal. Her mouth dropped open. "Married?"

He pulled on her hand until her face was inches from his. And even then, it wasn't close enough. "I can't live one more day without you."

"But I'm sick."

"All the more reason to enjoy whatever time we have, starting right now."

"But they'll split us up at Border Patrol."

"So we'll come home to each other every night."

"But..." She tried to think of a reason to say no, but found none. "Fine."

He raised one eyebrow at this. "A man proposes and that's what you say? 'Fine'?"

She leaned closer to him. "What do you want me to say? That my love for you will never die? That it took almost losing you to make me realize that you're the most important part of my life? That when I think about life after cancer that you are my bucket list? That it's you I want to spend every day with?"

He smiled, reached up and caressed her cheek. “Sounds like a good start.”

And so she kissed him.

EPILOGUE

THE NURSE REMOVED the empty bag from the IV stand and turned to Sherri. "That's the last one."

Sherri took a deep breath and smiled as the nurse slid the line from her port. "That's almost the best news I've heard lately."

"What was the best, then?"

Sherri lifted her left hand that sported a simple gold band. "That he loved me and wanted to marry me." She folded the blanket that she'd had on her lap and put it away in her tote bag along with the book of crossword puzzles she'd been using.

"Congratulations. On everything."

Sherri smiled again, then rose to her feet. She put the tote bag over her shoulder and opened the door. In the hallway, her family and friends had gathered with balloons and flowers. A loud hurrah started as she walked toward them. She covered her face with her hands. *What were they all doing there?* They were supposed to be meeting on the island of Belle Isle, a state park set in the middle of the Detroit River. She spotted Mama, who smiled and shrugged. "We all wanted to be here at the hospital on this last day."

Dez stepped forward and gave her a bouquet of sunflowers, her favorites and similar to those she'd held as they'd married the week before at City Hall. He held up his hands to quiet the group of at least two dozen well-wishers. "Before we celebrate Sherri's last chemotherapy appointment, I thought I'd say something to my cancer warrior." He put a hand on her cheek and looked into her eyes. "You are my strength. My hope. My love. Just as I am yours."

He kissed her and her eyes fluttered closed. She breathed him in and thought she could get used to this. Hopefully she'd have fifty years or more to do so. Dez backed away then put his arm around her, and told her, "I know we said that we'd meet you at the picnic, but no one wanted to miss this last part of your journey."

She concentrated on the faces of those who surrounded her, not just here in this hospital, but throughout her cancer diagnosis. She loved them all. Her parents. Her brothers and their families. April. Page. Her cousins, including Mateo. She put her hand to her mouth and blew a kiss to the group. "Thank you so much."

She started to proceed down the hall as they cheered each step for this last walk out of the chemotherapy ward.

The group left the cancer wing of the hospital and carpooled out to Belle Isle, where Sherri had rented a pavilion for the day. She and Mama had arrived earlier that morning to decorate the space with pink balloons, ribbons and streamers. As guests arrived, they brought covered dishes that soon filled one of the picnic tables. Mama had to get her brothers to pull over a second table just for the desserts.

Not hungry, Sherri moved around the pavilion to thank each guest for coming. Dez sat at a picnic table talking sports with his new mentee, Marcus. He reached over and wiped some mustard off the kid's face with a napkin. She went over to them and put her arm around Dez's shoulders. Marcus looked up at her. "I cleaned my plate. Can I please go and play volleyball with the other kids?"

Sherri glanced at Dez, who nodded. "And play nice."

"I always do." Marcus ran to the sandpit and joined in with the other children.

Sherri watched him go.

Dez laughed. "That kid's speed is always on full throttle. Does he even know the word *slow*?"

Sherri sat down at the place Marcus had vacated. "You're still thinking we should adopt him?"

"I couldn't dream of any two better parents that he could have." Dez rested his forehead against hers. "If the party gets to be too much, you just say the word and I'll kick everyone off the island. Or better yet, you and I can go home to bed. Leave everyone else to clean up."

"I knew there was a reason I love you."

"And here I thought it was my sexy bald head."

She stood and kissed the top of his head, then walked to where April and Page sat at a table with some of her cousins. Sherri put her arms around both women. “I don’t know how I would have gotten through all of this without my Boob Squad.”

Page winced. “We really do need to come up with a better name.”

April raised her red plastic cup of iced tea. “To Sherri’s last chemo.”

“To recovering from your surgery,” Page toasted.

April put a hand to her throat. “I can’t wait until you’re both at the place I’m at right now. To know that this is all behind you and you have a whole future laid open before you.” She raised her cup higher. “To the day we can all be in remission. And cancer is something in our past, but not our future.”

Sherri lifted her cup. “Hear, hear.”

* * * * *

Look for the next compelling installment of Syndi Powell's HOPE CENTER STORIES, coming soon!

And for more romances from Syndi Powell, check out THE SWEETHEART DEAL, TWO-PART HARMONY, RISK OF FALLING and THE RELUCTANT BACHELOR! Available today from www.Harlequin.com!